This Is Why We Can't Have Nice Things

ALSO BY NAOMI WOOD

The Godless Boys

Mrs. Hemingway

The Hiding Game

This Is Why We Can't Have Nice Things

Naomi Wood

MARINER BOOKS

New York Boston

This is a work of fiction. Names, characters, places, and incidents are products of the author's imagination or are used fictitiously and are not to be construed as real. Any resemblance to actual events, locales, organizations, or persons, living or dead, is entirely coincidental.

HarperCollins books may be purchased for educational, business, or sales promotional use. For information, please email the Special Markets Department at SPsales@harpercollins.com.

Originally published as *This Is Why We Can't Have Nice Things* in Great Britian in 2024 by Phoenix Books.

FIRST US EDITION

Library of Congress Cataloging-in-Publication Data has been applied for.

ISBN 978-0-06-339972-3

24 25 26 27 28 LBC 5 4 3 2 1

for

Cathryn Summerhayes

and

Francesca Main

thank you

Contents

Lesley, in Therapy	1
Comorbidities	29
Dracula at the Movies	53
A/A/A/A/	79
Peek-a-Boo	105
Wedding Day	133
Hurt Feelings	153
Flatten the Curve	187
Dino Moms	213
Acknowledgments	243

Lesley, in Therapy

Though their babies were very different ages, Lesley and Irina had returned from maternity leave at the same time: Irina had taken all of her allowance, plus holiday, but Lesley had cut hers short. This meant they were in the same session of Group Therapy for Returning Parents, which was the worst possible outcome for Lesley, because who wanted to attend group therapy with an ex-friend lost to the mom-zone? Plus, Irina knew things about Lesley that she didn't want anyone else to know.

The timing was bad. Lesley was pitching her new game to Jerry this afternoon, and Group (as the veteran mothers in the company called it) would take the whole morning. Ordinarily she'd have thought the chances of getting her game greenlit were positive, but she'd returned to a saturated market, in a slumped economy, with redundancies on the horizon. Frankly, it was a surprise Group was still running—but such was the power of Rise, the equal ops initiative distributing seed funding to the video games industry, which made training sessions like this compulsory.

Lesley exited the lift of IX Games at the sixth floor. It was a finance floor, something unsexy—maybe Procurement? Lots of dudes, anyway. The counseling room was through an annex, and the carpet—mole-coloured and furry—made her stacked heels sink. Irina was already there, as was Li Jing, who was on her phone. They were all recent mothers.

Irina smiled as Lesley took her seat. Since their mutual return Irina had been trying to reheat their friendship. "Funny that we're in the same session," said Irina.

"Yeah."

"How's baby Max?"

"He's good," said Lesley.

"Is he at Little Jungle?"

Lesley nodded. "And Zeppe?"

"With my mum."

"Nice to have family help," Lesley said, turning away.

The room was a homely space, especially for a building as high-tech as IX. It had the air of a doctor's waiting room, or a pre-mortuary; upholstered chairs, laminate signs, a plate of cookies on the table resembling dark, inert phones. Maybe, thought Lesley, sniffing the air for the lemon aerosol she'd once huffed in the high school toilets, they were in the cleaners' break area? She heard a sound, possibly from the radiators. A faint decay. Lesley wondered why they hadn't been put in one of the meeting rooms—but then they were glass-fronted, and she suspected there would be tears, dysregulation, feelings.

She was pleased to see that out of all the women here she looked the most put together.

It was weird that the therapist was late. Lesley had often been late to meet Christina, an unsmiling psychoanalyst of the classical school. Though it had cost her £75 an hour, Lesley had gently but consistently sabotaged the sessions. Anyway, she had long ago abandoned personal growth in favor of meeting the costs of childcare. Little Jungle did not come cheap.

Li Jing's phone was making whooshing sounds. She hadn't said hello, or even looked up as Lesley had walked in, and Lesley wondered if she too might be against all this. "Do you know how long we're here for?" Lesley asked her, but then the counselor bundled in.

"Hello, everyone! I'm Tina," she said, shaking their hands, apologizing about a stuck train at Moorgate. Tina's skin had a powdery silkiness to it, like latex. Under her scarf was a low-cut top, which, with her straightened blonde hair, gave her the racy aura of a late-night TV host.

Tina asked them to write their names on labels.

Lesley wrote "Les," which always stuck in people's throats.

"Right," Tina said, panoramically taking them in. "Quite a few of you have had babies this year!" She went on to talk about confidentiality, a safe space, what Group looked like, yadda yadda yadda, then, without warning, she launched into the session.

"What are your anxieties," Tina asked, "about coming back to work?"

Li Jing said managing her workload, and Irina said missing her connection with her baby, since she was still breastfeeding. Zeppe, she added, was fourteen months, and had started to bite.

Don't you mean toddler, Lesley wanted to say.

Tina turned to her. "Les?" Tina had that immaculately

generous air that Lesley always thought a great give-away of internalized anxiety.

Lesley lied, saying she had a bad back and her chair wasn't ergonomic.

"Lovely," said Tina, though she was obviously disappointed. "Sometimes, it can be helpful to reflect on where we have come from, so that we know who we are. Would anyone like to share their birth story?"

Irina was the first to talk, but Lesley had heard it all before and tuned out. Lesley and her husband had heard birth stories from new parents at the NCT group they had joined and swiftly left. The other couples had been unbearable, simultaneously sentimental but also domineering; Charlie had agreed they needed to be out of there, pronto. To the NCT leader they said they wanted to find a group in London with more Americans, but to each other they acknowledged the group's intolerable emotionality.

Now Li Jing—who perhaps would prove more willing to participate than Lesley had anticipated—was giving a synoptic précis of her first labor, which amounted to her campaigning for an elective caesarean the second time around, threatening her midwife with a self-laminated page of the NICE guidelines. Li Jing made a slicing gesture at her waist and then another, which was like throwing water from a bucket. Was that the baby coming out? "You think midwives are on your side, but they're not," Li Jing said. "They minimize your pain like it's *nothing*."

Lesley thought of her midwife, Sandra, who'd been very kind to her after baby Max had ripped her up good from V to A. The birth had made him impossible to carry. Imagine having a baby, and not being able to carry him! The thought made her feel so sad.

"Les?"

She could see Tina was trying to get in; Irina too was leaning toward her in a posture of active listening. It was like a game she might design; cat, mouse; reward, trap. "No," said Lesley, "thanks."

Lesley participated vaguely, and only when called on. An hour passed. The talk soon grew fetid with bodies and babies, and Lesley had to sit on her hands, just as she had at the NCT group.

Soon enough, Irina was crying. She used to be so fun, Lesley's drinking buddy, her pal, the person she WhatsApped about office gossip, but now Irina was almost entirely consumed by motherhood. "You know sometimes," said Irina, a rag of tissue in her hand, her face a baleful knot, "I lie awake with Zeppe in the night. My husband tells me to get *in* and get *out* of there, but when Zeppe is crying for me, *Mama, Mama!* I can't help but hold him. Sometimes, I actually get in the cot and fall asleep there. The next morning I'm so exhausted, and I have no idea," Irina gestured to the upholstered room, "how I am meant to attempt my new role."

This is why they'd fallen out with each other some months ago: it had started with an argument about Zeppe's sleep.

"You should never feel ashamed of giving your baby what he needs," said Tina. "You can't spoil a baby."

Irina's cheeks were red and her eyes were puffy. "My husband says we need sleep! That Zeppe doesn't *need* feeding in the night. But what can I do? I can't just ignore my baby!"

"I mean, you could," said Lesley.

Irina was looking at her, as if Lesley was better than this, and Lesley knew she was better than this, but still she couldn't stop herself.

As Tina talked, Lesley took in the scene. Here they were. From all of their bodies, babies had been born; bluish, bloody, a disco smell of iron on their vernixed skin. This was the only thing that held them together. And so what? So what if they had?

As Irina's crying turned into actual sobs, Lesley wondered how she might turn the conversation toward employment rights. Jerry had given her a full slate of client-facing jobs, though Rise suggested returning parents start off at 80 percent then be "phased" up to 100. If she could be on 80 percent, she could spend more time on developing new games.

"Is this right?" she said, interrupting Irina, probably at the worst possible moment, going by the way the others looked at her. "On the Rise model I should be on an eighty percent client load. My boss is trying to argue I am, but I was so overworked before I left they've actually just put me back on one hundred percent?"

"I'm not familiar with your company's policy," said Tina. "If we could focus on how your *feelings* affect—"

"Rise means nothing," said Li Jing, a biscuit crumbling between her teeth. "It also tries to get men to take their paternity leave, so, you know, ha ha ha. Who's your line manager?"

"Jerry."

"Yeah, so: good luck with that."

"Sorry, what's Rise?" said Tina.

"Rise is the equal ops and gender parity program," said Li Jing. "But it's a total hoax."

"How so?"

Li Jing swiped crumbs from the corner of her mouth. "You're not actually meant to ask for what it promises. And this is definitely not the time to stick your neck out."

Tina checked her watch. "OK, mums, let's focus on the here and now, and what we *can* change." She handed out mini whiteboards and markers. "Coming back to work from maternity leave can be joyful or challenging. No way of doing things is wrong." She asked everyone to write down four words describing their leave, without judgment, without censorship. Lesley looked blankly at her board and the ghosts of corporate language under it. She'd had two good runs at postnatal depression, and, after Max, Sandra had easily persuaded her back to work much earlier than expected.

Lesley had learned her truth: work saves.

She felt Tina's eyes sweep her empty board. "How did you feel you bonded with your baby, Les?"

"Fine."

Irina's eyes were still damp from crying, or were they welling up again, filmy with empathy? Lesley had told Irina about her postnatal depression: her inability to feel the love she wanted for her baby, which had sprung forth, so effortlessly, for her friend. With both babies Lesley had had a hard time. Charlie said she was being harsh on herself, but nothing seemed to come naturally to her, and she knew sometimes he pretended to be more negative than he actually was, just to make her feel normal.

"It must be very hard; wanting a career and wanting a family."

"Yep," said Lesley.

"Lesley, I think Tina's just trying to work out if there's some kind—"

"They're just babies, OK, they're not UFOs," said Lesley, letting the whiteboard pen press into her eyelid. "It's not *trauma*. We don't have PTSD. We have not come from a war zone. We are not *refugees*, or something. All we have done is have children."

"It can be a trauma response—"

"No—"

"To avoid the pain, to avoid the memory of what happened during a birth."

"No," said Lesley, almost shouting. "I just wanted—"

"Because trauma doesn't happen *in* language," said Tina, "it can't be expressed *by* language."

Lesley watched herself, also beyond language, as she threw the whiteboard pen at Tina as hard as she could. It bounced off Tina's forehead and fell on the nylon carpet.

"I just wanted to come back to work! OK! That's all!"

"Oh my God," said Li Jing, after a silence. "You just threw a missile at the counselor."

Irina looked at her aghast, but Lesley felt radiant.

Tina took a few moments. It was quiet aside from the whine of the un-bled radiator. There was a red mark where the pen had hit her.

"Les, could you pick up the pen, please?"

Lesley stood, dignified. She retrieved the pen and took her seat.

Tina rearranged her top and took a breath. "I'd like to dial down the emotion, if we may. Can I ask you all to close your eyes? We'll try a guided meditation. Can we think of our babies, and make them present, without guilt? Can I ask you, please, to do that?"

Lesley liked her anger, and didn't want it dialed down, but she also didn't know what else to do.

"Now I'd like you to substitute your baby with a golden light."

Lesley tried to imagine Max replaced with golden light, but he was too heavy for her imagined orb, and within seconds she opened her eyes and became distracted by where the hell they were again. This room made no sense: it was like a brown cave in one of the most modernist buildings in London. She thought of the song from *Frozen II* when Anna is in the cave, and she's alone and sad because everyone is gone; everyone is dead. Lesley's daughter, Emily, sang it all the time. How did it go?

"And let this light expand through your whole body," said Tina, "until it spills out and reaches the walls."

Lesley had watched the movie like a thousand times. The low-rent song of despair always made her cry, and as she watched Princess Anna stumble in the dark, without Elsa, without Kristoff, without even Olaf, she always had the same thought: I know this cave; this terrible cave.

All that heat, all that anger, replaced with sadness. Here she was, in this room: the old Lesley, deep in pain.

She could not cry. Tina would love that. Instead she felt her breasts tense and her bra moisten. "Oh, shit." She pressed down on her chest. "I'm not being disruptive. Not deliberately, anyway."

The other women watched her warily before they saw the two rings of darkening milk on her dress. Li Jing found some breast pads in her handbag. "Here. Have these," she said quietly, as if she too had been subdued by Tina's ionizing care.

"Sometimes your body wants your infant and you don't even know it"—Tina tapped her head, where the pen had landed—"up here."

"Right," Lesley said.

Wasn't therapy meant to make her feel better, more

optimized? Why was it making her feel so shitty? The plangent radiator had stopped its noise. "Sorry: can you tell me what this room is?"

"The room?"

"Like, where the hell are we?"

"Please!" said Tina, finally cracking. *"Please* will you just let us continue?"

But Lesley eyeballed her for the rest of the meditation, wondering how much Tina invoiced.

Restarting work had been a sensuous experience. On her first day back it was as if she were coming up. Lesley had seen other women—even the short-lived female CEO a couple of years ago—return to work like wounded Spitfires; a threat to themselves and others. Lesley had resolved to be different. She wore Scandinavian tailoring; she extended her eyes with liquid liner; she shellacked her nails dark gray. In the workplace she felt reassimilated. She had pictures of both kids tacked to her Mac: one of Max (held in "the Sandra") and one of Emily, happy on a swing. The photo always made Lesley think, with some astonishment, that she too used to be like that, a little girl, so idly inventive and wholly intact; a small person who hadn't yet had anything taken from her.

Because of her answers to the mental health

questions in the booking-in form, Sandra stuck around for weeks after Max's birth, quietly making sure Lesley was not having a breakdown. Charlie liked Sandra. Lesley liked Sandra. Sandra, a Jamaican woman in her sixties, with graying hair at the temples, was everyone's favorite person; mostly because whenever she came over Max magically stopped crying. Sandra had a way of holding babies, laying the spine up her arm with the head in her hand, which always calmed him. Even with Max, who was so heavy, she could do this.

(After that photo was taken, Sandra had discreetly made the sign of the cross over him, and Lesley, tears burning, had thanked her silently, because it might just give Max the protection he needed against his own mother.)

Colleagues had asked if everything was OK, given she'd returned to work so much sooner than expected. Lesley said she'd been bored.

Tina and Christina—the same name!—would think her attachment style highly ambivalent, but it had been Sandra—a woman who literally spent her life with babies—who said she was better off at work than wanting to dash the baby's brains out on the kitchen counter. "Don't worry," she'd said, "every mother at some point thinks about killing their child."

*

After Group, Lesley returned to her desk. She opened the package for her new game, "Air." The main graphic, a sphere, was colored in bitmap green. Gently she teased the sphere bigger. She knew from art school the relationship humans have to depth and shading; people genuinely thought "flat" animation lacked moral capacity. The game's central question was how to make the sphere big enough to float but compact enough to navigate the roads and buildings. Lesley dropped in the city footage. Now the sphere must be guided around skyscrapers and crowds without touching anything.

She played around with it, then texted Charlie, telling him she'd misbehaved at work, but he didn't reply. Charlie made mathematical models at an investment bank. Babies, he said, would make terrible data, because they refused to ever get into a pattern for very long. He was always very busy, and his work life had continued almost as normal between Emily and Max.

She turned back to the game: no narrative, no levels; "Air" was tend and befriend in the sweetest sense. The sphere's surface had a soft epidermal stretch. Even watching it in beta gave Lesley the feeling of pleasurable unavailability that she thought female gamers in particular would love, if only she could persuade Jerry, and the rest of the Exec, to resource her with a team. What people actually want, she thought, was absence. Thinking caused unhappiness. Not thinking was actually deeply pleasurable. The lure of a phone was that it was actually tantric. Her new game would offer, in the language of the nursery, the means to self-soothe. It was a bit kooky, but she could usually persuade Jerry on board. He used to call her the Office Wellspring.

Jerry had been a little distant with her since her second maternity leave. Sometimes he gave her this look as he walked past her desk: half pitying, half disappointed; like, where did my old gal go?! Where's my old wellspring?! What was the saying—one kid's a hobby, two's a chore?

Jerry's kid—Carla? Carlo?—also went to Little Jungle, but Carl(a)(o) was always perfectly contented, unlike Max, who, his key people said, often cried uncontrollably. Anyway, Carl(a)(o)'s behavior was—she told herself—symptomatic of psychopathy. She'd seen the "Strange Situation" on YouTube, and children who waddled into nursery without a backward glance at their parents could, decades later, just as well slay them in their beds.

Often she had to leave Max still crying on the

spongy floor. She thought it was bad to leave him like that, but in her haste to get to work she could never find anyone's arms to put him in.

As she finished the vertical slice she noticed the leaked milk had left doughnut shapes on her dress. Funny to think she had stopped breastfeeding months ago, and yet her body had chosen that moment to betray her. Funny, too, to think she'd thrown a pen at Tina's head, and, in the face of Tina's carnivorous empathy, she had not even apologized.

Lesley treated herself to lunch at Benoit's. Sexy people at alfresco tables drank tumblers of red wine, snapping breadsticks from paper holsters. Benoit brought her sparkling water. "*Signora,*" he said, ironically, because this was the part he played with other customers, not her.

Benoit was Senegalese, handsome, tall; a grandee of Charlotte Street, and he had a thoroughness that she always admired. For a moment she longed to take his hand, but did not. She ordered a plate of seafood. Over the linens Charlotte Street's lunch crowd packed into the restaurants and cafes. The office workers here were all so white, it was practically precolonial.

She used to come to Benoit's with Irina for boozy

lunches before they'd fallen out over text. Irina had been complaining about Zeppe's sleep, and Lesley—given Zeppe had been persecuting her friend for over a year now—had told her about "graduated extinction," where you left your baby to cry while gradually withdrawing support. It had made Max sleep beautifully, but Irina had been angry. Later, after indexing her sadnesses about Lesley's negligent parenting in paragraphed messages, which Lesley had to click "Read more" to finish, Irina had gone quiet, and Charlie had to restrain Lesley from replying honestly. She and Irina hadn't talked for a while, though she was making all the effort now they were both back at work.

She didn't think they were the type of women to have fallen out over sleep training. It didn't seem a big enough thing, but it obviously was, to Irina. Charlie often said kids made people become people they would have previously loathed. Lesley wondered if she had stuck with the therapy she might not have had to go through her postnatal depression a second time, which was not a rodeo she'd had any desire to revisit. She felt that if she had tried harder, she might have been able to prevent it.

"Where is your friend?" Benoit said, placing the antipasti on the table. "The Italian."

"Romanian. She's working."

"And how is your baby?"

"He's very cute."

The seafood suddenly appeared shockingly dead, like a Dutch still life; a mess of octopus, silky fish, prawns with anxious grins.

"Here." She showed him a picture on her phone.

He smiled at the photo of Max but looked mostly at her. "You're slim again. The bump was very big!"

Benoit, she thought, Benoit, the feeling cresting again that she wanted to tell him something. But Benoit was already at the next table, and besides, what could she say? After Max was born, I wanted to die? Worse, I wanted to kill my own baby? She couldn't tell a stranger that. In fact, she hadn't even told Charlie; only Sandra. Lesley looked at her big open handbag on the tiled floor. For a moment she thought Max was inside it, but then she blinked and he was gone. She remembered what Tina had said: about wanting your infant without knowing it.

Charlie finally texted, asking what happened. She told him about the therapist, and the pen, and the parabola, and he texted back with the monkey emoji, the one with its hands over its eyes. "It was probably her fault," he said, and she wondered if it was a good thing that he was always on her side against the world, but she took her reassurances where she could.

The seafood was so vinegary it made her mouth sore, and as she ate she felt sexy. Maybe someone would pick her up; leave a hotel key card on her table. That had happened to her once, a long time before Charlie, and the kids. It had been late, after work, and everyone had been drunk. The sex, in the mirrored room, with the faintly bullying Greek businessman, had been insane. The bedsheets afterward had been more disgusting than the ones on which she'd birthed babies; stiff with sperm from a man whose name, just now, as she placed a silver dart of anchovy onto her tongue, she could not remember. "What are you doing to me?" he'd asked in the hotel dark. Years later, Sandra had asked almost the same question of Max: "What are you doing to your poor mum?"

That afternoon, Jerry and the rest of the Exec were making her wait. This was fine: this was textbook. Through the glass wall she saw Jerry talking to CFO Steve, so named because there were two other white Steves on the Exec. The boardroom was outfitted in mahogany, with tubular steel chairs and black upholstery.

Jerry was always so casual in his attire: unzipped hoodies, dirty trainers; sometimes he smelled. She'd liked him, a long time ago, but after becoming a dad he was unbearable. He had, Irina told her, attended Group when he hadn't even taken any paternity leave. He always gave Lesley a raking smile at Little Jungle as they dropped off their kids with the Ryes, the Rivers, the Atlases, and she knew the smile meant: *I know it's Charlie's pay packet funding this*, before dodging away quickly, so that they didn't have to share the same tube carriage.

Finally Jerry waved her in.

"Hey, Jerry. Hi, everyone." She logged on to the presentation computer, and the guys woke their iPads.

Lesley pulled up the package, and, as the sphere inflated, her nerves disappeared and she felt the familiar feelings of beauty / mourning that had some roots in the eighteenth century. The sublime? Kant? Just as she was about to begin, there was a knock.

"Sorry I'm late."

Lesley looked up: Irina. What was Irina doing here? Her heart began to race. Was she here to tell the Exec that Lesley had assaulted the counselor? That she should be first in line for redundancy? But Irina took a seat near the window and pulled out her notepad. Irina, who was always so cheerful, hadn't yet smiled.

Jerry must have seen Lesley's confusion. "Irina's on the Exec now. Didn't you know?"

"No," said Lesley, trying to soup some warmth into her voice. "Congratulations."

"Thank you," said Irina, without looking at her.

"Irina's in charge of Product and Personnel."

"Right," said Lesley. "Of course."

"You gals all chilled after 'Group'?" said Jerry.

"It was cathartic," said Lesley, getting in there before Irina could answer. "I'll begin," she said, suddenly wanting this over. She launched the demo and began moving the sphere around the skyscrapers.

"So what's the loop?" Jerry said.

"The tension is: how big can you make the sphere, without endangering its safety?"

"Does it pop?" asked Irina. "If it touches something?"

"No. Think of it more as a flight simulator than an inbuilt set of VSRV."

"It doesn't get harder? Over different levels?"

"It's designed to get us out of language."

Lesley thought of the baby books that had promised a bond that went beyond language, and Tina, who said that trauma too was beyond language.

Jerry had that hungry-to-learn look, which she immediately knew was fake. "I get it," he said. "Like a Zen coloring book?"

She felt insulted that he thought her game was in any way like a Zen coloring book. "The only thing you must do is care for it. This sphere. It must simply be kept whole," she said, feeling oddly as if she might cry.

Jerry swiped his tablet. All the other guys were looking at her. "So it's a dot that you push and pull to varying thicknesses, that you take for a walk?"

His description made her think of manipulating her cervical mucus when they had been trying for Max. "Thinking is suffering," she said, watching, visibly, all thoughts fly from Jerry's mind. "Therefore 'not thinking' can be understood as a pure hedonic moment."

Jerry looked at her, expressionless.

"What's it called?" Irina asked.

"I thought 'Air'?"

"'Air'?"

"Yup."

"You know there's an 'Air' at Little Jungle?" Jerry said.

"No. I didn't know that."

Irina cleared her throat. "I don't think this one's for us, I'm afraid."

"I agree with Irina," said Jerry. "It's tough since you were gone. Much tougher. We can't gamble like we used to." He made a few commands on the iPad that she couldn't translate. "Are you having any more?"

"Ideas?"

"Babies."

Lesley looked at him, horrified. Was he allowed to even ask this? Despite Irina's new hard edge, she winced, and would not look at her.

"No," Lesley said. "No more babies."

For the rest of the afternoon, she watched Irina around the office.

Irina. Irina! Who had taken fourteen months' leave—*fourteen*—who was always taking mysterious breaks from her desk, who CFO Steve had once joked she would—if her husband let her—be a baby-making machine?

Lesley thought about the childish way she had behaved in Group. What if Irina thought she might act like that with a client? Like a person who actually assaulted someone if they couldn't get their own way? And what would she do if Irina made her redundant? She'd have to face the deep warp of mother-and-baby groups; nursery rhymes at the drafty church; coffee with the other mums she dimly suspected of criminal weakness, while Charlie worked in the seductive slipstream of productivity, math models, paychecks. *Irina!* Who had been so nice to her for the past few months, and whose sympathy for Lesley had now completely dried up.

Without any reduction in workload from Rise, Lesley had jobs to action: a tooth-brushing game for a chain of dentists; an animation for an architect's firm. But none of it interested her. Instead, she opened "Air" and did something she told interns never to do: she deleted it, and deleted its back-up too.

Lesley took the lift to Accounts. It had a brisk air that was lacking in Creative; an animating panic. Everyone was on the phone, talking up budgets, or trying to win new business. It hadn't been like this, before. She headed to Li Jing's desk. Her workstation was messy, and there were no pictures of her kids. "Hey." Lesley lowered her voice. "Do you know anything about the redundancies? Who they're going to cut?"

"No."

She sensed Li Jing was withholding.

"Percentages?" Lesley asked.

"I heard twenty."

"Twenty?" This was much bigger than she had imagined. "Is it the Exec deciding?"

Li Jing nodded.

"Irina?"

"Yup," she said. "Oh, by the way, I heard about 'Air.' Reminded me of that Sony advert? I thought it was a good idea."

"Thanks," said Lesley. "Is it illegal to get rid of someone after maternity leave?"

"No. Only during it." Li Jing gave her a once-over. "Oops! Should have taken longer." She smiled, but Lesley had no idea if this was a joke.

Back in the foyer, Jerry was waiting for the lift. She swerved toward the stairs but once there she didn't know where to go. Her desk? Home? Little Jungle, for an early pickup?

Instead, she found herself heading back to the sixth floor, to the carpeted hallway, to the therapy room and its fresh lemon scent. From inside she heard a rhythmic drone, then a gurgling, like falling water. She waited, listening, trying to work out what it was.

When she opened the door she found Irina, facing the window. There was a pump, shaped like a gramophone, attached to her breast, and she was swiping through photos of Zeppe on her phone. Lesley felt intensely but momentarily exhilarated. So this was the room for nursing mothers! She had worked it out at last! She almost wanted to tell Tina.

"Hi," said Lesley, coming into the room. "Am I disturbing you?"

"Not at all."

Lesley looked around. There was something about this room, something lyrical, emotional—was it the furnishings? The smell? Coming back inside provoked that feeling once more, that sadness, and she knew it wasn't for "Air" and its failure, but something else she could not name.

Irina's expression had softened. Maybe she felt sorry for her after the failed pitch, or maybe it was the flowing oxytocin. "Sorry about your game. It's a terrible market right now."

"That's OK," said Lesley. "I mean, whatever." She came deeper inside. "Congratulations. On the Exec."

"Thanks," Irina said. "It's a big challenge." She looked like she wanted to say more, but stopped herself.

"Was I awful to Tina?"

Irina shrugged. "Typical therapist. So nosy." Irina unsuctioned the pump, stacking the decanted breast back into her bra. She poured the milk into a bigger bottle, and attached the pump to her other breast. Lesley remembered how it had felt, occasionally, when breastfeeding Max: sort of wildly sexy but also deeply peaceful. She might have clung on to those feelings a little longer, but the desire to be on her own had been a bigger drive.

As the pump got going Irina said, "Did you get something from it? The therapy? At one point you seemed very moved."

"I did?"

Irina looked hopeful, as if Lesley had intended to come here to reclaim their friendship, but when Lesley saw Irina's hope she became determined to spoil it.

"I've forgotten what Jerry's baby is called," Lesley said, summoning this fact amongst the millions of more meaningful things she could have said. "Carl-a? Carl-o?"

"Carl," said Irina, sighing, her expression turning grievous again, and her long plait falling over her breast. "It's just Carl."

Lesley went over to the window. Six floors down, Benoit was setting the tables for supper.

"I thought you'd get the most out of it," Irina said, at last.

"Why's that?" Lesley said, turning back.

"Because you're the one who needed it the most."

Comorbidities

For a while Mason had wanted to spice things up in the bedroom. "If we don't make an effort now, there won't be anything left *to* improve," he'd said, and though I knew he was right, I was also tired. I spent all of my time with the kids. His work was crazy. Even sex once a week was an effort, and sometimes when we got into bed its warmth simply overcame us.

When I thought about our lives, I thought about the therapy pie charts on the internet, divided into slices of time: like, here's your pie for work, pie for sleep, pie for kids. I knew our sex pie was so thin it could barely stand on its own. All the websites said sex needed a bigger slice of the pie. They also said that if you don't have sex now, you can't have sex later—and I knew we couldn't stay on this minimal sex percentage forever, but we were tired! We were both so tired!

I used a lot of my pie on the kids. I think Mason was a little jealous of my romance with Aida (six) and Casper (one). Often, I felt lovestruck by my babies. Mason was always having to pull me out of their beds because I'd fallen asleep, generally communing, amygdala to amygdala. Sometimes, it felt as if both babies were still inside me. I had read that the Y-chromosomes of boy fetuses have been found in the bones of dead mothers. Once they are inside you, they are inside you forever, sweeping through you with a Coriolis force that went "I love you/you drive me nuts/I love you/you drive me nuts," which would bore down to Australia before you got to the end, and besides, it always ended with "I love you," because that's the way it went with your kids.

This is how my love felt for Aida and Casper: bone deep; viral.

A good chunk of my pie chart (like, maybe 8 percent) was spent tracking the global melt of the polar ice shelves according to the NASA website, which was a large percentage, particularly in comparison to the zero-point-something of our sex life.

My ability to worry about anything was capacious, even profound, though I personally could not see how anyone slept at night when floods, intensified storms, and freak supercanes were already bearing down upon us.

The other mothers at Rhyme Time could see it in me, this craziness, this relentless worry. They avoided me and talked with each other. I sang the nursery rhymes, but with very little heart. Sometimes I'd chat to them but it always ended up in eco-doom: "Do you think our babies have a future?" I'd say. "Will it be too hot to breathe?" They did not want to think about our babies' extinction. They wanted to sing "Old MacDonald Had a Farm," over and over, though the farm would be ashes; the animals, charcoal; and the MacDonalds and their kiddiewinks, burnt in their beds.

When Aida started to ask about climate change, I leveled with her: It's all our fault, I said, but mostly Granny and Grandad's: Cherry and Zhi-Sheng, her ma ma and yeh yeh. Then Aida would run around butt naked in the house screaming, "The world is on fire! The world is ON FIRE!" while Casper played with his new bottle, mauling the nipple with his teeth.

"Mason," I once said, in the middle of the night. "Do our kids have a future?"

"I'm asleep."

"I know, but I'm scared."

"You're always scared, whereas I have almost no opportunity to sleep."

This seemed too good to have been made up on the spot. "Did you practice that?"

"Maybe," he said, rolling over. I thought he really was asleep but then he said, "You need to de-catastrophize. None of this helps the world."

This is why I'm not horny! I wanted to say, the world on fire is not arousing! But in the morning I gave Mason a blowjob, as a way of saying sorry that I woke him, and sorry that our sex pie was so thin. "Thanks," he said afterward. "We needed that."

Mason was a celebrity mental health nurse. Day in, day out, he was saving the lives of all the teenagers butchered by the internet: its hateful gossip, its rancorous memes, its 24/7 bullying. He listened to teenagers talk him through their suicide plans, and then carried that pain home. Sometimes I read his Twitter feed to see what he was feeling, to trace the graph's curve of years spent in the NHS (*x*) and his personal sense of failure to the kids he had lost in his high-security ward (*y*).

That morning, the morning of the BJ, he put out the stuff for breakfast and whistled as he went. I wondered, if I had chimerically morphed with the kids, whether his brain might be equally comorbid with his dick.

We heard through the kitchen the sounds of our neighbor Kelly and her daily panicked descant as she embarked on the school run. She had four kids. Four! I'd told her I could only have as many kids as I had hands. "Otherwise they'd be raised by feet," she'd said, looking with darkening anxiety into the kitchen. Kelly was also very tired, but she always listened with sympathetic absence to my thoughts on the planet.

Mason was right, though. My catastrophizing wasn't helping. Aida's drawings showed the charred remains of lollipop trees, and when I looked at my babies there was a fiery orb around them, as if their aura recirculated the cognitive blazes I privately envisioned. Mason had asked me to please not discuss this with his mother, because these conversations always went badly, but one day Cherry somehow embroiled me in the discussion.

"If I stop eating pork," Cherry said, "the world is not going to suddenly get better."

Mason shot me a look. He had been at work for a long time; I could see the length of his shift in his face.

"No," I said, "but if *everyone* stopped eating pork it might."

Casper kept on yanking at my bra. I was sure I still smelled of milk, though I had stopped breastfeeding weeks ago. Probably it was glandular. Maybe I was secreting it.

"Squeezy's so hungry," Cherry said, which was the name she used instead of Casper. She picked him up and settled him on her lap. "Aren't you, baby?"

"Pigs fart," said Aida. "That's why the world's warming up."

Cherry narrowed her eyes. "I did not live through decades of Communism to be told what to do here. If you've eaten boiled shoe leather, you notice the pork in your porridge. Aida, come here and count Squeezy's fat rolls."

Mason's mother hated our choice of name for Casper. She said it had supernatural connotations. ("Because of the kids' movie?" "Uh-huh," she said. "Like the friendly ghost?" "Uh-huh," she said again.) Mason insisted his mother had a point, or at least that the point, however outlandish it seemed to me, was culturally sensitive. In Hong Kong, Mason said, there were massive holes in skyscrapers, like three apartments wide, for bad spirits to fly through—did I know how much that ancient suspicion could cost a real estate company? Tens of millions! Not letting ghosts into your house was worth tens of millions of dollars! Naming your child after an animated ghost was like inviting bad luck right into the crib.

The real problem with Cherry was that she was always right about everything. She'd swum from Shenzhen to Hong Kong to escape Communism, waded through the Mai Po marshes at dawn—and that was in the days when you'd be shot if caught. But I put my foot down on the Casper front, insisted it was a name I had long cherished (who knows) and as a result Cherry always gave him less lai see than Aida at Chinese New Year, which was weird, because he was a boy, and, you know, etcetera . . .

"It's their future," I said, emotional, "that's why I'm concerned."

"Hey," said Mason. "Are you crying?"

"I'm not crying."

Since stopping breastfeeding I had felt very emotional. Perhaps I hadn't been ready, but Mason had this idea that when the baby was a year old it was time to let them go. In truth, while feeding Casper,

I had never felt sure of my boundaries. There had been merge. Ontologically, I had felt synthesized. I'd loved it, and at the same time felt stranded by it.

"It's the milk," said Cherry, "it's coming out of your eyes."

"It's not the milk coming out of my eyes."

Cherry looked at me and crossed herself. She had hedged her bets, and was now both a Taoist and a Baptist. "If you have another baby," she said, "then you can feed that one too. Mason said you're sad about stopping."

"I'm not sad. I'm fine."

Cherry desperately wanted us to have a third child. Perhaps it was because she herself had had only one.

"There are already too many people in the world," I said.

"Nonsense." She looked at Mason. "Poor Mason, you look so tired. Why don't I take Squeezy too next Saturday?" she said, actually winking. "When was the last time you were by yourselves? You can have a date night!"

"I don't think so," I said, before Mason could agree. "Squeezy can take the bottle now."

"That would be wonderful," said Mason, before I could offer another protest.

When Cherry had gone, Mason cracked open a beer. Casper was threatening to run a black crayon up the wall. When I took it off him he started to cry, then attacked Aida, clawing at her face. Then Aida tripped him over, and his wails filled the room.

"Enough!" said Mason. "Time for bed! Everyone!"

"It's four o'clock," I said.

"Then why aren't we watching TV?" he said. "And no *Topsy and Tim*, OK? That shit has very toxic gender roles."

I thought about what a good mood he had been in after the blowjob and how he hadn't whistled for weeks. As we settled on the sofa, I said, "How about a home movie on Saturday night?"

"Sure," he said, laughing, as Topsy made cupcakes with Mummy, and Tim drove his toy 4x4 across the savannah of their Astroturfed garden. "See you there, Ms. Kardashian."

About seven bajillion years ago Mason and I met on a dating app dominated by aggressively randy men. I'd been sent tons of dick pics, which sometimes made me feel horny and sometimes grossed me out. Sometimes I got into extended sexting conversations where I'd take nude pictures of myself and they'd send laughably priapic photos, which I'd then reverse Google Image search to see if they had been cribbed from the internet. Sometimes we'd have phone sex that would end with an insane orgasm but also the astral distance of strangers who didn't love each other, who didn't know each other, who didn't even know if the other's profile photo was real; though sometimes it was this very nothingness that made the exchange so arousing, like having sex with a zero, or a bot, or yourself.

Any hope of a relationship was useless. It was like whamming your head into the crotch of all these dudes, giving eight hundred blowjobs, and asking for nothing back, and I knew the delinquency was only a front to hide my inner, terrible longings for intimacy.

So when I started messaging Mason I found his sincerity almost anti-normative. As a public-facing mental health nurse, he had half a million Twitter followers @PoetParamedic. He had warned me, over the app, that he was Chinese, like *fully* Chinese, and that when some white women met him they were disappointed. He was in turn surprised when, at the tail end of our first date, he found me so wet for him. Suddenly, at twenty-seven, I had felt for the first time the total vortical tension of falling in love, and I remembered with some regret the austerity of all those unnumbered dudes with whom I'd done so many nothings, so many times.

Mason was quieter than the other guys I'd dated, and 1,000 percent more sensitive. Often, when I fucked up, like when he was recording a live segment for TV at home, and the kids swarmed into the living room as I was scrolling Instagram in the kitchen and didn't notice after five—then ten—minutes, he was more or less instantly forgiving. He lived with the theory that with no ill will there was never any responsibility; the kids he worked with were proof of this. Given world history, I personally thought this was a bad argument, but it was one I accepted.

The next Saturday we packed Aida and Casper off to Cherry's. We would reunite for Sunday lunch at Jade Garden, but for the next twenty-four hours, both kids were gone. Instead of being anxious, as I thought I would be, I felt joyful. There was a sense of festivity in the house, as if we were both on holiday.

I told Mason that I had great things planned for us, sexually, on our first kid-free morning, but in the meantime, we would sleep. We hadn't slept through the night for twelve months, and that night we slept cadaverously and without interruption. When we woke there was actual daylight peeping at the curtains, and we marveled at the fact that nobody needed anything from us.

For a while I looked at Mason's body; the sexy line of hair from his navel to crotch, his slender frame that hid his strength. When he was in his scrubs he looked even better because I could see the faint outline of his penis, which seemed, to me anyway, like a failure in tailoring. I kissed him on his chest. I could tell he was close-eyed-thinking rather than sleeping. I whispered: "Do you want to make that home movie?"

He opened his eyes. "I thought you were joking."

"Why not?"

I could tell he was surprised. For most of my pregnancy and Casper's life, I had stopped initiating. I knew it frustrated him that I no longer wanted him like he wanted me. He understood—we both understood—that our inability to care for each other was because our burden of care was so large—but it didn't mean he wasn't sad that this part of us had so quietly died; a part of us that had once been so raw and lurid.

"We've got to be careful," he said. "Paris Hilton . . . Kim Kardashian."

"Weren't they on purpose? Didn't they actually

release them?" I shifted onto my back as he played with my nipple. "Also Hulk Hogan."

"Hulk Hogan what?"

"He released a tape."

"Did he?" He scrunched up his nose. "Gross."

Mason abandoned my nipple and read a blog about digital security and home movies, then went downstairs to fiddle with his laptop: turning off the Cloud, putting his searches on private, clearing his cache and browser history, then turning his phone to airplane mode.

He was right to be paranoid. A few years ago, his Twitter account had been hacked, and the hackers had taken Thai ladyboy faces and pasted them onto pictures of him they'd found in his Photos folder, with racist captions in shadow box lettering saying things like "Yin Yang, suck my dang." Otherwise he got sent messages saying "Why dont u kill urself," or a pasted menu from a Chinese takeaway, or they'd send videos of themselves wanking during his Teen Mental Health slot on CBBC.

When Mason came back he put his phone on the pillow, flipped the viewfinder, and toggled to video. I wondered if I should have tidied my bush but it was too late now.

"Are you sure everything's off?"

"Sure."

"We're not on Instagram Live?"

"No." He showed me the phone's airplane mode. "Imagine we're inside the plane, forty thousand feet from the world, our family, the kids."

Knowing I could kibosh this whole thing with my anxiety, Mason started kissing me, and slowly I began to switch off my worries. At first, we couldn't look at each other without laughing. But when I watched the video I stopped thinking. It was pretty hot. I was turned on by Mason's lips and the way they were mashed by my own. When he took off my T-shirt I watched as his lips moved the nipple around, kissing and licking me.

Casper had favoured the right boob, and it was noticeably bigger than the left, but I tried not to think about the kids. I wondered if I would feel weird about my post-pregnancy body, but it looked OK: the boobs had more sag, there was a cradle of fat hip to hip, but mostly it was fine. Mason's body was still pretty much the honeymoon it was in his twenties, which wasn't fair, but it was at least mine to enjoy.

Mason sat me on top of him. In the video we watched ourselves intensely, which might have proved monotonous but was very arousing. We came quickly, and I pressed the red button immediately to stop the recording.

We cuddled, then Mason went to the bathroom. When he came back he twinned his phone to Bluetooth, and I listened to the lonely submarine pulse of the speaker trying to find its pair. He began a mellow playlist I hadn't heard in a while. Soon I realized it was the playlist he'd made for the birth of Casper, though he must have forgotten this. A Brian Eno song began playing, and Casper's labor came back to me: the abrasion; burn; rip; a flow of blood; then everything went dark, as if I had died—but instead a baby was placed on my chest; a heavy thing with a mineral stench.

Mason was sleeping now. Over the song I heard the rhythmic loop of the bathroom's extractor fan. I felt a little sad. The sex had been nice, kinky; a return to form. It had a lustiness we'd once taken for granted. But something in me felt empty. Only now that the kids were away did I realize how much we had both lost, the price we had paid. I thought I was about to cry, but instead I saw Casper's breast begin to gently leak milk against the pillow.

The windows of Jade Garden were tinted, as if to ward off great shelves of subtropical light, and inside the air was hostile with air-conditioning. On some tables there were pristine cloths and spotless lazy Susans; on the tables recently vacated, a general wreckage of tea leaves, bones, towers of dim sum crates, and the general atmosphere of a raid. Through the aisles older women pushed trollies, picking up empties as they went.

When I saw my children, sitting nicely for their ma ma and yeh yeh, I felt things that were hard to admit. I wanted to preserve who I had been this morning, and not go back to being these good people of endless patience and infinite care. I looked at Mason, panicked, not wanting to say goodbye. He kissed me. I guess he was thinking the same thing. Then we went over to them: our old frontier.

Zhi-Sheng's nose ruffled when I kissed him hello. Even with the faintly aquatic smell of prawn in the air, I could still smell the bedsheets on us. He was filling in the dim sum docket. "Are you still vegetarian?" he asked.

"Pescatarian."

"What's that?"

Mason placed his phone on the table provocatively. I looked at it and looked at him. "Only seafood," he said. "And fish."

"What's the point in that?"

"Fish don't fart," said Aida.

"Exactly," I said, putting her on my lap. I looked at the outline of Aida's face, and the fineness of her features, her overwhelming beauty.

"Can we play 'Silly Lady'?" she whispered.

Aida loved playing Silly Lady. It involved me pretending I had absolutely no idea who she was, and that I had to take her to a police station in order to find her real mummy. It only worked if we played it in public—that was the point—there was a longing in her to feel publicly disowned, which might, I guess, be universal. Often she went berserk, saying "Mummy! Mummy! It's me!" as she jumped into my eyeline, but I would disavow all knowledge of her, and one time she had laughed so hard she had wet herself, as if her bladder could not handle the queasy uncertainty of not being mine.

"Not now, darling," I said.

"Did you profit from the morning?" asked Cherry, a glint in her eye.

"We just watched a movie," said Mason, suppressing a smile. He tapped his phone with a finger. "We'll probably watch another one later, too."

"Squeezy was so cute. He filled diaper after diaper! When are you going to potty train him?"

"Next summer," said Mason.

Crates of dumplings arrived: rosebuds of siu mai, winter melon bao, and some wonton that Cherry scooped out for Casper. As I watched Zhi-Sheng dunk his bun in soy sauce, turning its milky whiteness the color of wood stain, I realized I was ravenous. Everything Cherry put on my plate, I ate; even the chicken feet. Zhi-Sheng said something in Putonghua, which I guessed was "I thought she was pescatarian," and Mason just shrugged, and smiled at me for miles.

Zhi-Sheng had to order more. He had a long conversation with one of the trolley ladies while Cherry visibly yawned; he was always flirting with the waitresses, getting a little drunk, and flushing with beer.

Aida put one of the bamboo crates on her head, and said, "Look, I'm Ma Ma when she was a peasant!" and I swatted the crate away before Cherry could see. More food was brought. Because of the video, and the energy I'd put into it, I felt so hungry. On and on I ate, and I thought: I could do this all day. I could do this all day!

"Are you pregnant?" Cherry asked quietly.

"Ha, ha, ha," I said, through a mouthful of dumpling. "Ha, ha, ha."

"You know, I couldn't conceive in Shenzhen. All that sweet stuff in Hong Kong—the dan tat, the peanut butter pancakes!—that's finally what made Mason."

"Or maybe you were less stressed?" I said, eating the chicken foot the way I had learned from her, with my lips closed and my mouth laboring. I extricated the bones, and said: "I can't imagine the shoe factory was very . . . nourishing?"

For years Cherry had made knockoff Michael Jordans at a factory in Shenzhen that specialized in perfect counterfeits. She returned my gaze. "No. Freedom did it."

"How was church?" I asked Aida.

"A man was in the water and another man had to pull him out!"

"He made such a loud noise!" said Cherry. "So dramatic! Like he was drowning. You're meant to fill in the form if you can't swim."

"I can swim," said Aida, with some expectation.

"You can wait till you're eighteen," I said.

The talk went Putonghua, and I tuned out, tranquilized by the MSG and happy to remove myself from the grown-up conversation. Repetitively I fetched whatever morsel Casper threw to the floor; Mason watched Aida spin his phone on the table. I finished off the food, while Casper had a meltdown, struggling with his strong limbs to get out of the high chair, nearly knocking it over and smashing his face in.

I imagined us in the famous scene from *Don't Look Now*, where Donald Sutherland and Julie Christie have sex, intercut with their musing about it afterward. In my reconception, it was with two spacey parents responding to their children in the restaurant. And the audience would think: haven't they done enough! Don't they deserve a longer break?

I looked over at Mason, who was also lost in thought. I wondered if intimacy was fleeting, or whether you had to constantly make it. Most of my friends thought I was lucky to be in love with my husband after kids. A friend's husband now actually slept in a toddler bed, because their youngest boy would howl, "I'm lonely, I'm lonely!" in the night, and they'd dozily swap places at three in the morning. So yes, I felt lucky, but also . . .

I looked at the bones on the table. What had I done? Why had I eaten all this animal? I shivered. I felt crazy, and unlike myself. Maybe I was doped up on sex, or MSG, but the mood was not unwelcome. There was an air freshener a little way off, and I tried to pace how long between intervals it took to spray its pine scent.

"Mason," I said, and he turned to look at me, but

I didn't have anything to say. He took my hand, and Cherry nodded to herself, as if in confirmation. The table was now clear.

"I'm glad you've broken the curse."

"She's not pregnant, Ma," said Mason, exasperated. "We told you. No more babies."

"Why not? Look at Squeezy!"

We all turned to look at him. With all the attention on him Casper beamed, then leant over and bit me with his hard, ridged gums.

"Two is enough," Mason said, as I prised Casper off me.

"Two is no better than a pair," she said.

I didn't know what this meant.

"Cherry's always been baby-mad," said Zhi-Sheng. "That's why she loved Mason too much."

"You can't love a baby too much," I said.

"Yes, you can," Zhi-Sheng said, and then he watched his wife, to see how she would react.

After lunch we went to Hyde Park. Mason went ahead with the pushchair and his dad, while Aida walked with me and Cherry. The day was bright and glossy, and the trees, heavy with blossom, were shaken by mild winds. The heavy refrigeration of Jade Garden was beginning to thaw, and all the cultivated nearness of the restaurant had dropped away.

"Is Mason OK?" asked Cherry.

I knew it took a lot for Cherry to ask me this. "His work is exhausting," I said. "The caseloads are bigger. The work is more complex."

"We could take them on a Friday night too?"

"Then he just wouldn't ever see the kids."

She nodded. "I show the ladies at Bridge the videos of him on TV. They're so jealous, but they don't know how tough it is for him."

"It's hard." Though I knew she wouldn't understand, I wanted someone to talk to. "We say: here's the internet!" I gestured to an imaginary esplanade. "Poke around, kids, but it's like a dungeon in there? Rape porn, bullying, one-dollar bikinis"—I counted them on my fingers—"beheadings, hacking, child abuse—often from each other. I mean. This is what he listens to. This is what is on his mind *all the time*."

Cherry nodded but looked vacant. We passed the Peter Pan statue, with the rabbits and children coming from the black rock, and I thought of our neighbor Kelly, with her kids swarming her skirts. "I grew up in a village," she said. "I have no idea." Cherry looked at the sculpture plangently, as if it hid all the children she had never had. "So you're not pregnant?"

"Nope."

We carried on to the Serpentine. The light had a satiny bounce off the water, and Cherry popped on her Ray-Bans, which made her look fantastic. "I never liked her," she said tartly as we reached the Memorial Fountain.

"Princess Diana?"

"What a whiner. If I was a princess, I would have enjoyed myself!"

Mason and his dad had already crossed the river, and I saw Cherry gaze at them fondly. In the push-chair Casper had nodded off, his absurd curls crowning his big forehead. Zhi-Sheng waved and blew a kiss; maybe the amatory result of the lunchtime beers.

Aida ran over to the bridge. As I watched her, I thought of our video in the future, joining the deadly slime of the internet that had made all those teenagers' lives miserable. The thought of someone leaking the video onto some democratic porn hub made my face burn. Imagine if the kids, one day, found it, and watched it! I thought of Mason touching the airplane mode to show me his phone was off. When he'd done that, had he accidentally turned it on again?

I felt intensely panicked, and texted Mason on the other side of the river: delete the video.

I saw him look at his phone. Three dots appeared as he wrote back.

The air had gone gummy and chilled, and a wind gusted through the trees. I turned, looking for Aida, who was now up on the bridge. She couldn't see me, but I could see her. *Over here!* I wanted to say, the Coriolis force barreling through me. *Aida, Aida, I love you!* While we were in the shade, she was in the last of the sun—and the radial flames tore around her head.

Dracula at the Movies

Vassily had rung her once already this morning and was now calling again. Ray knew he was calling to give her directorial advice: strategies to get her way with Cedric, the DOP, and with Ivy, her capricious lead. She hated when Vassily gave her advice; hated it even more when his advice reassured her.

Vassily was Ray's best friend from film school, but his beautiful movies only made Ray feel shitty and tired. She longed for both the critical and commercial success he so easily generated. Plus, she found her envy mortifying: she couldn't admit it, not to anyone.

Despite herself, she forced herself to call him back.

"Riri!" Vassily said. Ray—Rihanna—*Riri*. "How's *The Disappearance*?"

"Weird," she said. "Everyone's behaving themselves."

"That's good, isn't it?"

"Yes," she said, and then: "I don't know."

"You don't know?"

"I mean . . ." She wanted to hold back from confessing her insecurities, yet the crew would not tolerate vulnerability, and the desire to unburden was strong. "Everything's going so well, what if it all falls apart? The weather is beautiful: sunshine, every day! And Cedric—can he have *been* this abstemious? I haven't seen one woman crying yet. And the baby is fine," she looked down at her bump, which seemed to have grown overnight. "She's just floating around; getting on with business. And when I think about getting through the shoot intact, well, the hope, really, is worse—"

"You need to relax," said Vassily. "Enjoy. It's your third film. The third is always the best. And Ivy: *dis moi.*"

"Ivy is sober. Ivy sober is one hundred percent a basic bitch. Instead, she's kind to everyone, nice to me. What's wrong with her?"

"Oh, don't ask me. I have no idea why you insist on working with her."

Ray had been treated to Vassily's Ivy lecture too many times to hear it again: that her obsession with Ivy was wrongheaded; that Ivy could be replaced by any number of up-and-coming actresses who didn't smoke, drink, or at random times self-administer what she liked to call "ketamine therapy."

"You're not a pre-Raphaelite, you know," Vassily said. "This is not the Brotherhood. There are other actors."

This was Vassily all over: always talking in French, or referencing art history, or citing recherché Soviet films no one had ever seen. Anyway, Vassily was pretty two-faced: Ivy's confidant when all three of them were together, her critic when they weren't.

"I have to go," Ray said to the velvet hotel room. "Ciao, Vassily. Don't be a stranger," she said, but he had already hung up.

Rationally, he was right, of course. Insurers too had been sceptical of Ivy: citing her drug use, her erratic persona on Twitter, Lahore, and even her dead twin as evidence of her unreliability. Ray still had flashbacks to the day Ivy—possibly in a K-hole, and certainly during the apex sex scene of Ray's second film—hadn't stopped meowing like a cat. Ray knew all of this, and yet her desire to shoot Ivy felt both emotional and ancient. Ivy was Ray's muse, and muses were not to be chosen. *Meow*, Ivy sometimes teased her now, offering her claws. *Meow*.

The Disappearance was a mass-market thriller. Ray had pitched it to the producers as *Sleeping with the Enemy* meets *Rebecca*, and the budget had been beyond her wildest dreams. If it established her name as a director of suspense she'd never have to beg for money again. Over the next few days they would film the climax: essentially an extended chase sequence, where Ivy showed the most fear. In prep, Ray wanted to get into Ivy's inner emotional core, which inevitably meant heavy talk about the dead twin.

In *The Disappearance* Caroline (Ivy) has faked her own death to escape an abusive relationship with her husband (Trenton) and is now hiding out in a mansion in the Surrey hills. Today they were filming the moment where the viewer realizes the husband has found his way into the house, and the camera, essentially, becomes the stalker. The second unit would later film inserts—close-ups of buttons, a photograph, a wedding ring: everything the husband touched—but for now Trenton would be hiding under the bed as Ivy, unaware, went about getting dressed.

In the bedroom Kharmel was finishing Ivy's makeup, and Cedric was directing his gaffer to catch the near-white filaments of Ivy's curly hair.

"Where's Trenton?" Ray asked.

"Under the bed already," said Matthieu, her line producer.

Ray laughed. Really, the patience of young actors! She found Trenton's face staring at her from under the bedframe, and saw something of her own devotion in his expression. "Hi, Trenton."

"Hi, Ray."

Soon Costume wanted her to choose between two identical white shirts. Hair wanted to change Ivy's style because the same styling in every shot was "boring" instead of normal. Then Matthieu wanted to merge this scene with ninety-two—which he might be right about, tonally—and Cedric wanted to know how much of Ivy's ankle would be shown if the camera was, for the most part, under the bed. And was Ray really insisting they needed a close and medium shot from two angles, which would necessitate a change in the lights?

She did insist. She got to insist.

Ray loved this: the questions were exhausting, yes, but the feeling of mastery was exquisite. She entertained all of these things all of the time, even while going to sleep at night, and they weren't a burden, but a pleasure.

"How are you, Ivy?"

"I'm good, yeah," said Ivy warmly.

Kharmel was applying the last flick of liquid eyeliner.

It was underhand, possibly ethically dubious, but Ray planned to do Miskar's paradigm later today to stir up Ivy's negative emotions for tomorrow. Ivy's twin had died in mysterious circumstances: circumstances Ray dearly wanted to find out, not just for tomorrow, but for Ray's future biopic about Ivy's life.

Freddy, her boyfriend, who she was surprised to find a deeply moral man, would think this exploitative, possibly even re-traumatizing, but Ray knew all directors traded on their actors' histories to amplify their on-screen performances. In fact, she knew of one director who'd basically treated his lead—a very famous actor, who would engage in cocaine parties with multiple prostitutes—like total dogshit, just to reflect back the relationship he'd had with his abusive father. And the actor? The actor was soft as putty on the set, totally malleable, and had later won a BAFTA, expressing his gratitude to his father/director in his gushing acceptance speech.

"Remember," said Ray to Ivy, "Caroline's lost her fear at exactly the wrong moment. At the moment of utmost peril."

"And you want me to show that with my feet?" Ivy said, looking, incongruously, at Ray's belly.

"Just show me your happy feet. Happy-go-lucky heels and toes."

"All done?" said Cedric.

Kharmel blushed. "All done."

"Why do you think Ivy's in such a good mood?" Ray said quietly to Matthieu, as they waited for Cedric to choose his lenses. "Is she in love?" Ray asked. "Maybe Ivy's in love. With Cedric?"

"Please, God, no."

Cedric had narrowly missed out on being MeToo'd and was trying hard to sleep with only one person at a time. Ray wondered why her luck had come all at once. Was it the baby? Did it function as some kind of magnet for the universe's good vibes?

"I saw a book about therapy in her handbag," said Matthieu. "Maybe she's processing things."

"All that stuff with her twin," Ray said. "So much trauma to work through." She added quickly: "I imagine."

"C'est pas ça." Matthieu was from Réunion, and always got cross when Ray talked about Ivy's dead

twin, and when he was cross he spoke in French. "Kharmel says it's the baby."

"The baby? Why?"

"It makes Ivy want to be nice to you. Or she wants one herself. A little *bébé*." He looked longingly at Ray's stomach. Maybe he was thinking about a family with his boyfriend too.

Ray loved working with Matthieu, and she worried that Vassily would poach him after the baby came. Matthieu and Vassily were friends, so it wasn't impossible. Vassily's new movie, *Lantern Rising*, was a black-and-white number, which was just so typical—so classy—something so beyond what was financeable for her. Whenever she thought of Vassily—who swept his haunted, Cold War charm across so many awards rostra at the age of thirty-eight—her envy felt basically like arsenic. But also, she had to admit, a little animating, a little like fury, because with each of Vassily's successes she became more determined to outdo him.

Yes, envy was the operational blueprint for everything she did. Another friend—not in film—had once told her a Buddhist proverb that urged you to wish *more* success toward the person whose life you coveted. Ha, ha, she thought.

Ha, ha, ha.

*

Ray had yet to make a film without Ivy. She'd been obsessed with the twins since she was a girl, covering her room in posters of both Ivy and Cora. When Cora died, at thirteen, it had felt like Ray's first experience of grief, though her parents couldn't understand why she was mourning a girl she'd never met. But Cora's death had pushed like a cold front through her brain, and it felt as though that chill had never left.

Sometime in the future Ray wanted to make a biopic about herself and Ivy. It would be a beautiful film: a feminist metafiction about directing, women, muses. About losing someone, and how replacements were found for those who'd been lost.

The arc? After the death of her twin, Ivy is in a wasteland: a bereaved child actor who can no longer work. Her savior? Ray, who rescues her from oblivion and relaunches Ivy's career. Together they produce stunning films about making art in a man's world. And when Ray had found out she was having a girl, she figured her daughter could play Ray as a child. The biopic would be so pleasing, so cyclical.

And so much free press!

How do you feel about playing mommy as a girl, sweetie?

Yes, Ray's and Ivy's lives were so intertwined that it would be impossible to ever separate their futures. A while ago Ivy would have been shown in magazines with an inset photo of her dead twin and a line or two about the family tragedy. Now, it was Ray who took Cora's space. Yes, theirs was a relationship worthy of some Latin or maybe biblical pronouncement: *Whither she goes, I follow*.

In the garden, Cedric was setting up the next shot behind Ivy, who was dressed now in a gray silk tracksuit. This marked Trenton's first arrival at the house. The grounds were lovely: bright green with ancient plants swaying in the icy April light. Though it was freezing, the sun shone with unerring reliability, and would be gorgeous for the final outdoor scenes of the next few days. Maybe it was the sunshine improving Ivy's mood. Vitamin D. Maybe all winter Ivy had been SAD. Or *had* SAD? Anyway, long may it last, since for the whole shoot there'd been no powder around Ivy's slender nostrils, or whiskey on her breath, and it boded well for *Darkness as a Bride*, their fourth and subsequent film together.

The cool thing in this scene was that—Ray had stolen this from a French film whose title she couldn't remember—Trenton wouldn't be in the shot. The audience would guess that he'd arrived just by the persistence of the camera on Ivy's face. Presence via perception. Cedric would set it up as static and wide, and the shot wouldn't change for over a minute. The audience would feel resistant—why isn't there a cut?—until they understood that the camera was Trenton; Trenton was the camera.

And the audience would be delighted, creeped-out.

"The light is too flat," Cedric said. "Why is it always sunny? Check out the angle, will you?"

When Ray saw the image in the monitor she could imagine the audience's reaction in the dark of a multiplex. For a moment, she had an image of herself nursing a baby in an altogether different darkness; the baby nipping as it sucked. Really, she had no idea what she was getting into. When she thought about her future as a mother, she was afraid—and the fear wasn't the cool high notes of cinema terror either, but something altogether less contained.

"It's good," she said, but Cedric continued to fuss.

Ivy lay on a sun lounger. Her curly hair fanned around her face like a white fire.

"Just go somewhere inside yourself if you can, Ivy," Ray said. "I know it's hard. But the audience needs to be as perturbed by your stillness as the stillness of the camera."

Technically, Ivy was a tricky film actor to direct—she could be late, or high, or drunk, or worse (*meow*)—but truly, she had exceptional talent. After three or four takes most actors went dry, but Ivy could explode into the scene every time. And she knew how to hold it, too, between takes. Hold it, then repeat it. "You OK?" she said to Ivy, who hadn't moved.

"Oh yes," she said. "This is my forte. Being nothing."

Ray almost felt bad. Here was Ivy, so tranquil, and in an hour or so Ray was about to shit on everything by exorcising Cora. "Meet me in the cafeteria after this, will you, Ivy? I have an exercise for you to do before tomorrow."

Just then, Ray's abdomen turned hard and she had to count her way through a Braxton Hicks. It was weird, like Ivy had made it happen; invisible, anticipatory vengeance: as if they too were in a horror film. But soon it softened, Ivy remained still, and Cedric shouted "Ready!"

At film school Ray had a semiotics teacher from Hungary called Professor Miskar. Professor Miskar had explained that horrors might be usefully divided into two categories: Frankenstein horrors

(=left-wing), which dealt with the horror within, and Dracula horrors (=right-wing), which focused on the menace outside. (Basically: over there, Transylvania.)

Dracula horrors, he said, were easier to make. Anybody can spot a predator, an alien, an external threat. But Frankenstein horrors were harder, because they relied on the director and the actors to really know the monster within themselves.

Professor Miskar asked them to think about their own inner monster. Was it self-serving? Greedy? Vain? Envious? ("You see," he said, "why *SE7EN* was so successful?") He asked them to write about the worst thing they'd ever done; something that to this day still caused them shame.

Ray sat, paralyzed. She watched Vassily scribble away, hopelessly purgative. Instead of writing something truthful, she made up how she'd poured boiling water on a cat, or something. Then they had to write something terrible that had happened *to* them; the Draculean thing. Honestly, she could think of nothing more tragic than her most recent breakup, and she longed for something genuinely traumatizing that would give her the legitimacy of a real storyteller.

Which was the true horror, Professor Miskar asked

them afterward. Was it to perpetrate the evil? Or to have it perpetrated upon them?

The class sensed the correct answer, but Miskar was a severe man and no one said anything. What a dumb fuck, Ray thought in the silence: no one but the most privileged white dude would ever think that experiencing horror was in any way preferable to perpetrating it.

Vassily raised his hand. "To perpetrate the evil," he said, "most definitely."

And Professor Miskar smiled.

Bingo.

Ray watched Ivy as she walked through the cafeteria. She was a tall woman with pale skin and hair the color of the moon. She gave off an almost ambient glow. That's why she played so well in horrors, Ray thought, as Ivy sat: she was already otherworldly.

"How are you?" Ivy said, touching Ray's stomach.

"You know you're meant to ask if you want to touch it."

Perhaps Kharmel was right—it *was* the baby improving Ivy's mood.

"Oh, whatever," said Ivy. "She's practically my baby too."

Ray had no idea what this meant.

"Baby," Ivy said, putting her hand on Ray's stomach again, "kick once if you think I'll win an Oscar."

Baby did nothing.

"Sleeping on the job," said Ivy.

Ray looked for a sign that Ivy might be high, but there was nothing.

"So," Ray said, "I thought we might try a thing. An exercise." Ray knew she had to go about this delicately. "The film of course paints Trenton as the monster. But in each scene there's a transmission: Caroline's part of the dynamic. She's made the relationship as well as him."

Ivy cocked her head. "I always just thought of her as the victim."

"No," said Ray. "It can't be that simple."

Ivy pulled out her notebook, which was a cute addition to her new willingness to learn, and began to take notes. Ray had the desire to look in Ivy's bag to see if the therapy book was still in there.

"So Caroline arcs into strength, but first she has to leach some of that monstrosity from Trenton so that she can destroy him. Caroline is scared she's going to die, or, worse, be existentially subsumed into her husband's identity. That's why she has to pull on her own bad energy before she can kill him. She has to find her own inner monster."

Ray searched Ivy's clear face, the wide-set eyes, the beauty that made her think of the towering Vivienne Westwood models she'd shot in music videos after film school while Vassily was having his first feature green-lit. Maybe that's my monster, Ray thought: my envy.

"My teacher at film school," continued Ray, "told us about this Dracula / Frankenstein thing. I think he called it a paradigm? Anyway, it's where you meditate on the worst thing you've ever done to someone else," Ray said, feeling a thrill at being so near the no-go zone, "and the worst thing someone has done to you."

Ivy's pen was poised above the page, looking at her: the cellophane eyes, the smiling mouth collapsed. "The thing I feel most badly about?"

"Yes," said Ray.

"The worst thing? The worst thing?" Suddenly tears sprung. There was a silence before Ivy spoke, completely choked: "No, Ray. I'm not doing that. This is my life. OK? It's not yours. It's not yours."

The next morning Ray was in her hotel room, waiting for Vassily's phone call. He would be itching to lecture her on Ivy's exquisite sensitivity, advising her not to ever use Ivy's private life to charge the scenes—which was ridiculous, knowing what he got up to with his actors. And now, all day, she'd have to deal with Ivy's bad mood, and the baby had gone weirdly sideways, overnight, so that Ray looked as if she'd swallowed a shelf.

Within minutes Vassily's name appeared on the screen. To speak to Vassily would take a great deal of energy, but to ignore him would take more.

"Listen, Riri, no bullshit, eh? I saw Ivy yesterday. You *have* to stop asking her about Cora."

"I didn't."

"She said you used Miskar's paradigm."

"It was an exercise!"

"She doesn't want to talk about that with you."

"I didn't ask her about Cora!"

"Riri, you are not Polanski."

Ray held her head. "Why would I even *think* I'm Polanski?"

"Hey, don't have your baby, OK?! Just cool it on the memoir stuff."

The wind against the speaker sounded rough, coastal. Vassily was scouting locations for *Lantern Rising*. She knew his schedule. "How's casting?"

"It's OK," he said. "It's fine. It's great, yeah!" This

was typical Vassily: neutral to exhilarated in three adjectives, so that she wasn't even allowed to know if things were harder for him than they looked. "I have to go," he said. *"Ménage bien l'actrice,* Riri."

Then he was gone. She didn't want him to go, and yet she didn't want him to stay on the phone either.

The hotel room was dense with stuff: chairs, cushions, carpet. She felt like throwing or snapping something. Instead she bit hard on the viscose curtain, and saw, with some pleasure, her teeth marks in the cloth.

Despite everything, Ivy seemed fine that morning—cheerful, even—as they prepared for the moment when Caroline, in the bath, realizes the game is up: her husband is in her home. Noises, banging windows; frights, chills and jumps.

The shot was laborious (they always were when dealing with naked humans—especially women—in cooling water), but Ivy was professional. Maybe a little remote, but that made sense after the fumbled paradigm, and Ray wondered if Vassily had been stirring, just to psych her out.

Despite approaching Ivy several times, however, with the express intention to apologize, Ray just couldn't get it out, and then she got waylaid by an unexpectedly tearful Kharmel.

After she'd controlled Kharmel's emotions they eventually got the shot, and Ivy brought her lunch to Ray's trailer as usual.

"What will you do for childcare, when the baby comes?" Ivy said, a pink flake of fish balanced on a fork tine.

"Fred will do the first bit. Then a nanny. *Bride* will be December. So I have to be ready for that."

"Has it moved?" Ivy said.

Ray thought Ivy meant the film schedule but saw she meant the baby. "She went sideways this morning. I can't get her to *re-jig*. It's not great, to be honest." Unexpectedly she felt tearful. It was Vassily: getting to her. "Sometimes, I feel like I'm host to a parasite." She felt sorry for herself, and decided to use her pregnancy to provoke Ivy's sympathy. The sentiment was true—the host thing—but it wasn't, in particular, bothering her right now.

"Well, you look perfect," Ivy said, kindly. "And it'll be over soon."

Ray felt pleased at this unasked-for intimacy, and decided against apologizing: Ivy would just think she was trying to insert Cora into the conversation again, and then there'd be another earful from Vassily.

For a while, Ivy concentrated on her food. Ray wondered if—as Matthieu had suggested—Ivy was either pregnant, or wanted to be. Ivy had only ever dated throwaway London boys whom she'd picked up at parties, but that didn't mean she didn't want all this.

"I've been thinking I might retrain," Ivy said tentatively. "You know. Maybe do a course."

"In what?"

"Psychotherapy?"

Ivy had mentioned counseling before, as an alternative to her acting career. But Ivy was always threatening to quit, and never actually did.

"No way," said Ray. "You think people could tell a famous film star their problems?"

Ivy looked down. "Maybe you're right."

Ray watched Ivy eat the salmon skin, which made her feel nauseous. She remembered Vassily's cute lecture. Ray realized, then, that she hated Vassily—her best friend from film school; she utterly hated him. And if she was looking for an antagonist in the biopic, it would be him.

"If you have a girl," said Ivy, "will you call her Ivy?"

"No," said Ray, laughing.

"My mother was an actor's assistant. Then she had twins. You never know what's going to happen, do you?"

"I'm not having twins."

"Sure, *you're* not having twins."

Ray thought Ivy would continue but she didn't.

"You know my mom signed me and Cora up for modeling at the age of two? *Two?* That was just to get us out of the house. Modeling was like free childcare for her."

Ray acted like this was all ordinary, but for Ivy to have even brought up Cora was highly unusual—indeed, Vassily had said it was all but out of bounds. "What was LA like"—ventured Ray, wishing she could take notes, because she needed all the biopic info she could get—"as a child actor?"

Ivy tensed. "I don't remember that much of LA. Most of my teenage years were in London."

When they'd finished their lunch Ray made them both coffees, then they went outside so that Ivy could smoke. The sun was out, but the clouds were stacking. Ray tried to hold her silence. She knew this was what journalists did to make people speak.

Ivy lit a roll-up. Ray thought it sweet that Ivy rolled her own, as if she couldn't afford straights.

Matthieu radioed, but Ray wanted a little longer. She was about to close a deal: maybe even get something new on Cora.

Then Ivy began talking, as if continuing a conversation, and Ray realized she was answering Miskar's question.

"We were on set," Ivy said. "A horror: I don't remember the title. I'd hurt my wrist. I'd climbed a tree and fell. Anyway, the director had asked Cora to take my place on the day of the car accident. Because it wouldn't work to have me in the scene with my wrist already bandaged. No CGI, back then. And there was already an identical actor lined up to do the job for me."

Ivy picked a thread of tobacco from her lip.

"After Cora died, I played her role so that the movie could be finished. *Quid pro quo.* They paid me Cora's fee, as well as my own. My parents were happy. Suing the studio was going to be expensive. During Cora's scenes, I just felt completely blank. As if I was neither Cora nor myself.

"That's what I feel most badly about," she said. "In your Dracula exercise. That it was meant to be me in the car that day. Not her. That's the thing I can't bear. That's what I hate most about myself."

Ray had known Ivy had acted Cora's role after her

twin's death, but not that it was meant to be Ivy in the car that day.

"It must have been terrible," Ray said, her voice a little flat with the cliché, but she was trying hard to mask her excitement: this secret would be a huge reveal in the biopic—possibly the climax.

Ivy cocked her head. "Isn't that what you always wanted?"

"What?"

"To know about Cora. My guilt. My shame." She opened up her palms. "Everything."

Ray thought she had kept her interest, all of this time, somewhat casual.

"No," said Ray. "I mean, only because I'm interested in you. And only because I care." She watched as Ivy rolled another cigarette. It was unusual for her to smoke more than one, but the stress was obviously acute. "How did you decide to go back to acting?" Ray asked, in a voice she imagined would be like a therapist's. "In your twenties?"

"I didn't," Ivy said. "You took me hostage."

Ray gave this a beat. It wasn't as if Ivy hadn't had a choice. Modeling was boring, Ivy had said, in one of their last adverts together. She'd wanted more, and Ray had given it to her. "Did Vassily say something to you, Ivy? He called me this morning. He said I'd upset you."

Ivy looked straight at her. "You know he's casting for his lead?"

"Yes?"

"He wants me for *Lantern Rising*."

"Oh." Ray felt a fire in her chest: an ignition. "When's the shoot?"

"December."

Ray's mind scrabbled. "But what about *Bride*?"

"You'll have to find someone else. I don't want to be in your movies any more, Riri."

"What? You're leaving me?" Ray didn't know what was happening. Her muse? Abandoning her for Vassily? And just as Ray was about to have a baby! "For Vassily? But he's so . . . awful."

"Better than this. Anything would be better than this."

The smoke rose from Ivy's cigarette, and Ray noticed whitish flakes falling, and she thought at first it was the ash from Ivy's cigarette. But then she saw it was everywhere: an early April snow, falling from the sky, tinged blue, as if in a watercolor.

Cedric's voice buzzed over the radio: "Ray? RAY? Are you seeing this? WHAT THE FUCK IS ALL THIS SNOW?!"

In the background of the static there was the sound of someone crying—maybe Kharmel again.

And then came another one of those awful contractions; the hardness of her stomach repulsing her. Vassily. *Vassily!* He'd finally betrayed her, fucked her over 100 percent, as she'd always known he would. How could she find a new lead between the baby and the shoot? A new lead of the same fame as Ivy, *and* with a newborn in tow?

Just then the baby maneuvered: a hand pushed out from Ray's stomach, and Ivy's expression went from happiness to horror. Then the baby settled into her old position, and the feeling was like a release.

Ray made a promise to herself just then: the first actor to be cast in the biopic would be her daughter. Ivy was the most private person she knew. She would hate the biopic, and also be incapable of stopping it. The revenge felt cold and calculating and deeply appealing. Ray would make it at all costs, whether Ivy was in it or not. *Bride* could go to hell. Fuck Vassily. Fuck Ivy. She'd start writing the biopic as soon as *The Disappearance* wrapped.

"That's fine," Ray said, smiling at her former lead, as the snow began to settle on the bright green grass. "That's fine, Ivy. I wish you all the very best."

A/A/A/A/

Even though Gaël and I were separated, I felt upbeat about the future of our marriage. Every couple of weeks, when he came back from Paris to see our girls, we found it impossible not to make love. Recently, he seemed happier: like he cared about life again. Paris had given him time to reset. I could see that in a few months, or by next year at the latest, he might be ready to come home.

Looking after the kids by myself all year had been hard, though. Whenever I was feeling down my best friend, Marissa, would console me by doing impressions of Gaël in her shitty French accent. "Bah, I am Gaël, and I am so sad! So mise*ra*ble!" Marissa at this point would rake her high black hair away from her forehead to mimic Gaël in the tallest peaks of his almost constant melancholy. "Do you want me to do Béa, too?" she'd ask. Béa was Gaël's mother, a psychoanalyst, and the person, I believed, most responsible for Gaël's *angoisse*. Béa had not been in touch with me since our breakup. Not an email; not *un petit texto*.

Marissa was older than me. She'd split from her very wealthy ex some years ago, though Sancho still sent her money, and they continued to share ownership of their cat, Patty, whom they called their baby. Patty lived mostly with Marissa, and had very expensive veterinary bills. Sancho spoke with Marissa almost every day.

There was talk at some point of them getting their *decree nisi* but neither Sancho nor Marissa had done anything about it, and, in the eyes of the law, they were still married. Marissa even had a boyfriend, who might have put an end to this relational indeterminacy, but Hector was in LA (a venture capitalist) and he and Sancho didn't have much to do with each other.

Hector said to Marissa—at least get a will. No *decree nisi*, fine, but a will is a bare minimum. He said if she died intestate everything would go back to Sancho. Marissa didn't want to get a will—fear of death, or talking about it, or something. Finally, Hector said: "What happens if Sancho gets a new girlfriend? And your money goes to her as well as him?"

"Ha," said Marissa, "as if."

Eventually Marissa decided she'd get the will. She wanted a fancy law firm in the City, but I persuaded her that a poky solicitor in Camden would do the same job.

The solicitor introduced herself as Ms. Barber and shook our hands.

Ms. Barber asked about Marissa's assets.

"There's my flat in Tufnell Park," she began. "I own it outright."

The flat had been a gift from Sancho after the separation.

"Liquid assets?" Ms. Barber was making notes on her legal pad in a casually private style. "As in: cash, rough total."

"Two hundred thousand."

I must have looked shocked because Ms. Barber stopped writing. Only two years ago Sancho had given Marissa a million so that they could be financially free of each other.

Marissa did not look at me, but added, both as caveat and explanation: "My flat needed work."

"Dependents?"

"Two kids. But they're all grown up. Ninety-five percent, split fifty-fifty."

"And the other five percent?"

Marissa turned to me. "That goes to Stacey. But just her. Or her girls, if she's kaput before me. Not Gaël."

"Who's Gaël?"

"My husband," I said. "Or ex, maybe."

Ms. Barber wrote down Gaël as "Gail" and then scratched out his name; then she wrote down Sancho's and scratched that out too.

"Patty will go to Sancho. Patty is our baby," Marissa said, adding: "baby cat."

"What about Hector?" I said.

"Who's *Hec*tor?" said Ms. Barber, looking tired of us already.

"Hec*tor*," said Marissa. "Oh, I don't know." She looked abstracted. "Our days are tonally opposite. He lives in LA. It's hard to get into a conversation that doesn't get bogged down in binaries: 'I'm going to bed / I'm getting up.' 'I had a bad day / mine hasn't started.' 'It's too cold / it's too—'"

"So no Hector," said Ms. Barber.

"No Hector," said Marissa, tossing her hair. "For now."

*

After the appointment we went to a concept store on the high street almost entirely dedicated to plants. The shop had the warm misty smell of a Victorian glasshouse. There were vibrant mosses fed off micro-nutrient jellies, Japanese bonsai encased in bell jars, and tanks of exotic fish that darted with multiple lightning streaks this way and that in folding and refolding shoals. I had a desire to put my face into the crystalline water to feel the pump's aggressive bubble.

Marissa was excellent at spending money, but I still couldn't believe she'd pulverized Sancho's lump sum so efficiently.

The electric pink jellyfish in one of the aquariums illuminated her expensive skin. "Sometimes it feels as if Sancho is this big boat," she said. "And I'm try-ing to swim away but I keep getting dragged back in the wake."

"Do you mean romantically?"

"No," she said, laughing. "Not like that."

"Financially?"

"Not quite, though yes, in all likelihood. Do you think Sancho has cut me from his will?"

"I mean, probably."

Sancho was a contracts lawyer, or tort; hostile takeovers, or something else vaguely menacing I could never remember. His job was one of the reasons they'd split: he'd never been around. "Like being married to air," Marissa had said. He was fiscally clever. There was no way he hadn't thought about ring-fencing his personal wealth.

"Do you think I should have made provision for him? For Sancho?"

"No," I said. "What does he need provision for? He's fine. He's rosy."

Marissa looked pained as she watched a jellyfish propel itself forward. The water looked fake: CGI. "You know, you get married, expect things; then instead—this. It's not quite the dream, is it?" She picked up a price tag, dropped it. "My dad wanted me to be like that woman. Ms. Barber."

"A lawyer?"

"I think he thought a clerk."

I lost Marissa to an anteroom, and as I walked around I thought of my own marriage and the way the dream of it had been diminished. Over the years—and since children, more specifically—Gaël had often escaped to Paris to check out of family life; but each time, bar the last, he'd come back. I understood he compromised my feminism by being so selfish, but at the same time I loved him, and just wanted him home. I guess in the past year

I'd learned my principles were weaker than my feelings.

Marissa bought an enormous jar with layers of colored vegetation: soil, grass, some succulents on top with bluish vines. It cost £400. She paid on her Amex.

"It'll last forever," said the sales guy, who looked like he might spend £400 on a haircut.

"Like a love affair," Marissa said elliptically.

"Two hundred left, though?" I said, as he bubble-wrapped the jar. "I thought Sancho gave you a million."

"I mean, at my age you can fritter that away in just a few years. A few things here, a few things there—then, poof!—all gone."

"Don't you know it," said the haircut, and Marissa took a second to absorb his intervention.

"What happens, though," I said outside, "at the end of the two hundred?"

Marissa waved off the question and ordered an Uber. "Shall I get it to school? I love picking up your girls. The look on their faces"—she fireworked her fingers—"totally sparks joy."

While we waited we sat by the mother-and-child fountain. The mother's breasts were golden where passersby had fondled them, and because of some plumbing problem the woman was always crying. Whenever we passed, Lila would steal a kiss from the mother's mouth, then she would talk to the statue, sometimes for minutes. I always felt taken care of in that moment, because I knew Lila was telling the statue how much she loved her, and therefore how much she loved me.

"How are you?" Marissa asked, in a meaningful way.

I said I was fine, and Marissa breathed through her nose. She got annoyed with me for not talking about things, for not showing emotion.

"Listen, Patty has to have a procedure," Marissa said eventually, as we climbed into the Uber, which smelled of synthetic pine and cigarettes. "In Paris, next month. It's on her eyes, to clear the ducts."

"Why Paris?"

"The surgeon is the best in Europe. I'm paying for the train. Sancho's doing the bills. Will you come with me? Girls' day out. Also, I need help with the French."

"To Paris?"

"My treat," said Marissa, looking out of the window as London gentrified northward. "Granny can pick up the girls and we'll be back before teatime. Can you organize work?"

I hadn't been to Paris since our split.

"Sure," I said. "OK."

Though our children had certainly made Gaël's depression worse, he'd forgotten that he'd also been a wholescale pessimist long before parenthood. When I'd first met him—bearish, bearded almost up to his eyes—he'd seemed wounded, hurting, which I put down to his recent return from Baghdad. He had been a translator for the Americans, but it turned out he'd only ever worked in air-conditioned rooms that still smelled of new upholstery. In Iraq he'd started lifting weights because he said Baghdad—or the Green Zone, anyway—was immensely boring.

At first, the sex—by dint of Gaël's purgatorial haunting—was kinky. He threw me around. We did everything to each other, and, as he sat on my face and I licked out his asshole, I wondered if this was what it felt like in his heart: watching the darkness descend with only seconds to gulp for air.

It was only later that I realized his anxiety had far predated Iraq. He said his depression, which had started when he was a teenager, had been untouched by the therapies his mother had paid for, and Béa had despaired about her professional inability to help. And at some point, Gaël's anxiety about his failure to overcome his anxiety had become even bigger than the anxiety itself.

What was strange was that to everyone else—in London he worked at Al Jazeera—Gaël projected tranquility and even imperturbability, but in the evenings it was down to me to deal with the toss and roil. He wanted to talk to me, to me only, but eventually—after Andréa, then Lila came along, and after our sex life had all but been replaced by sleep—it was useless; like trying to talk someone out of diabetes. And he started spending more time in Paris.

I urged Gaël to go to the doctor. I talked about chemical imbalances, circuitry, motherboards, all that stuff, but he said pills would zombify him, and he told me to please stop asking.

Then he left for Paris and didn't come back.

At that time Andréa was learning about repeating patterns at school and had been taught to translate the real world into basic algebra. Soon we found repeating patterns everywhere: the clock's tick/tock, the radiator panelling—A/B/A/B. One day in spring, deep into Papa being gone, Andréa noticed a streetlamp switch from dark to light and back again. "A/B/A/B!" Then, after a moment, she said to me: "What is Papa?"

"*What* is Papa?" I was very tired. Her face was

open and beautiful. I thought of Gaël's individuated pattern of misery. "A/A/A/A," I said.

"Non," she said. *"Il va à Paris/Il reste à Londres/Il va à Paris/Il reste à Londres. C'est* A/B/A/B."

"Oui," I said, as the lamp mysteriously stayed on black. *"T'as raison."*

A couple of weeks after making the will, I bumped into Sancho outside Marissa's flat. It was early. Marissa had ordered the Uber to take us from here to the Eurostar.

"Oh, hello," Sancho said. He was highly strung; he carried his stress in his shoulders. "Where are the girls? Aren't you at work?"

"They're at school. I'm waiting for sign-off on a job."

He cleaned a fingernail with his car key. "I don't understand what graphic designers *do*. What do they do all day? Why are they so expensive?"

I already understood this to be a rhetorical question, because I'd told him the answer once before, and Sancho never really listened.

"This surgery won't actually change anything," he said. "Patty will go blind eventually, whatever happens." He looked even more stressed than usual and I wondered what was up. "Here's the address."

He put his phone on top of mine as if paying for something. When the details appeared I saw the vet's was in the twentieth, which was Gaël and Béa's *arrondissement*.

"Tell Missy"—his name for Marissa—"I said goodbye. OK?" He looked at her sash windows. "She never was my animal." He pressed the fob, and his car lit its greeting. When he shut the driver's door it closed with an SFX sound like a movie set in space.

Marissa's flat might be described as sterile but the absence of children's things provoked in me the same feeling as walking into a spa. There was something ambient about her wealth; it made me feel part of it.

"Are you ready?" I shouted.

"Yes!" she called from her bedroom, but didn't come out.

I sat on the sofa in the living room. On the coffee table there were thick interiors magazines and an opened envelope branded with the solicitor's office logo. I didn't notice Patty until she jumped on my lap. Marissa had chosen the carpet to match Patty's coat, and the congruence was striking. Because of Patty's breed, and the shape of her skull, her epiphora—the almost constant overflow of tears coursing down her face—left puddles everywhere, and it was this incontinence that meant Marissa had to change her carpet almost biennially, and which Sancho paid for.

I wondered what Sancho had been doing here so early. Maybe they'd been having sex. When I thought Sancho had looked stressed, maybe he was actually just tired after a long night of banging his ex.

I wondered if there would be enough time to see Gaël in Paris today. Probably, there wouldn't be enough time, and, anyway, I hadn't told Marissa about our little affair, fearing her disapproval.

Whenever Gaël came to London, the expression on his face—parenthood lightened by the visitation privilege—made me feel as if I'd surfaced a small hill. Whatever python-like grip his depression had had on him had been released. Was it Paris that had done that? Space from the kids? Space from me? Our new sex life? A radical new therapy? He had talked of EMDR: of releasing his story (his absent dad, his overbearing mother) through his eyeballs.

When Marissa came in, Patty jumped off me. The tips of Marissa's hair were wet from the shower.

"Are you sure you can't get this done in London?"

"Stacey, this guy's the best. The best. The internet insists."

"Have you got your passport? And Patty's?"

Marissa scooped up the cat and cradled her. "My baby." She dabbed the cat's forlorn eyes with a hanky. "No more tears. No more." I watched her gaze travel to the solicitor's envelope. "Did you open that?"

"No."

She dropped Patty abruptly, and went to look out the window. Sancho had long gone. "Oh no," she said. "Oh no, no, no."

Patty hardly made a noise all the way to Paris. Marissa was pensive on the Eurostar, and then the Métro. Sancho wasn't replying to her texts. She should have told him about the will beforehand, she said. He'd not cut her out of anything; he'd only ever been completely generous. Now she'd gone and done this. "I feel like I've set things in motion," she said, with a look of dread, as a repeating metro station flashed in her eyes.

We got off at Alexandre Dumas and headed to Rue des Orteaux. For central Paris the twentieth was down-at-heel, though it had its flashes of wealth. The tower was a modern building, and the vet's was at the top.

We sat in the pale green waiting room until the nurse called us to a side room, where she indexed the possible consequences of Patty's surgery (blindness, paralysis, death), which I quickly translated. As I talked, I saw the tension build in Marissa's jaw. Patty mewled.

The waiver Marissa had to sign was in French.

"It all looks OK?" she asked me.

"You want me to read the whole thing?"

"I'll just sign it. OK. I'll just sign it."

Outside the tower block Marissa moved a tear from her eye. "What if Patty dies?"

"She won't die," I said, though an image of Patty dead in the catbox surfaced violently.

Marissa looked at her phone again. "Still nothing from Sancho."

"Look, the will doesn't actually matter unless the tunnel caves in. Nothing's changed!"

Marissa put her face in her hands. "Everything's changed.

"Sancho's ruthless. How do you think he made so much money in the first place? How do you know he hasn't changed his will first?

"What if he cuts me off? As a punishment. For showing such a lack of trust, of respect?" Her face went pale. "He could just stop the credit card."

"He'd give you a warning. He's not a monster."

"Imagine if I had to go it alone," she said, almost laughing.

"I think you need to eat. OK? Have a meal. Forget about Sancho and Patty. Let's just eat. Pick up Patty. Go home."

Back at the Métro there was a covered market with stalls selling cheese and fish and vats of submerged olives. Women in hijabs and athleisure and old men with wheelie bags did the marketing. Under the canopy there was a powerful scent of good produce. The funny thing about Marissa was that despite her good taste and her ambulatory wealth, she wasn't bothered by food. Often, at dinner, she could settle for an egg.

We headed to a café I knew, but as we were walking I noticed a woman coming toward us. I realized, as I put the bits of her together—the auburn hair, the blue eyes, the generous breasts—that it was Gaël's mother.

"Stacey!" Béa said. "What are you doing here?"

As she kissed me she held tightly to my arms.

"My friend's cat is having an operation. Her eyes."

"Your cat? You must be nervous."

"Oh!" said Marissa. "I'm beside myself! She's my baby really."

Béa cocked her head. "I'm Béa. Gaël's mother."

"We met at the wedding," Marissa said.

"When do you pick up your cat?"

"In a couple of hours."

Béa turned to me. "*Vous mangez avec moi?* I haven't seen you in so long." She squeezed my arm again. "We are still family. *T'inquiète pas. Gaël travaille.*"

I had a sudden desire to understand what Béa knew about us, and I thought Marissa would enjoy the haptic adventure of Béa's beautiful home, so I said yes. Soon we were following my mother-in-law through the gated mews. Her house had been a former newspaper press, and Béa had preserved its ironwork features. The furniture was mostly antique, but there were also highlights of very bright and expensive plastic.

"Oh!" said Marissa, "I love this!"

"*Merci,*" said Béa, as we came into the kitchen. "How old is your cat?"

"Six. She's a Persian Blue."

"I hear Persians can be problematic." Béa took a quiche from the fridge. "Sorry. Not very interesting. I thought I was eating alone."

"I don't know what I'd do if I lost her. I'd die."

Béa nodded. She seemed in a warmer mood than usual.

"Where do you practice from," I said, "if Gaël is here?"

"I have outside premises now. Much better."

"Is it nice to have your son at home?" Marissa said.

"Of course. But he misses his kids."

Béa poured tumblers of white wine and cut generous portions of the quiche. As we talked, the wine made the conversation diffuse. There was a long conversation about schooling in France and England, then housing, then the rubbish on Paris's streets. "Do you have a lover?" Béa asked Marissa, swerving. "A man, or woman, in your life?"

"My husband and I are separated. But I have a boyfriend. In LA."

"Being apart from people you love is very hard."

"Yes," said Marissa. She had never told me she was in love with Hector. "Maybe I will marry him. Then I could see more of him."

"Eh, it's one way of doing it." Then Béa said, almost impishly, "Look at us. Three women without their men. Wouldn't you say we are thriving?"

Marissa blinked. "Thriving," she said. "Yes." I saw anxiety flash across her eyes, and I wondered if it was about Patty, or about Sancho's discovery of the will.

Béa patted her on the wrist. "You'll see your kitty soon."

Béa asked about the operation, and Marissa

explained the epiphora, the cat's constant crying, the drainage of the *lacrimal puncta*. She said the vet had come recommended via online forums. In one post she said a woman had described the surgeon's hands in great detail—their fineness, their superior softness—and how it was only this surgeon who could be trusted with an operation of such delicacy.

"Gaël seems better," I cut in, the wine making me feel bold.

"Doesn't he? Like his old self!" said Béa. "He puts it all down to an antidepressant, but he doesn't see how much he himself has done. How ready he was. I think it was his emotional work that did it, not the pills."

"He went to a doctor?"

"He's on some Paxil." She steepled her hands. "I think it's created the conditions for escape."

"Escape?"

"Like Houdini! Escape from all the dysphoria."

"Well," I said, "good," though I felt wounded; that he should be finally doing all this without me. "He's been miserable for decades," I said, in order to hurt her. "Since he was a child."

"Probably I shouldn't have told you," Béa said. "Probably it's private."

I felt myself tearing up but pushed the feeling

down. Rain hit the windows and left its own scattered pattern of tiny dots. I felt confused and also ambushed—hadn't this been what I had wanted? For him to be better? But why hadn't he told me? And why hadn't he done it when I'd suggested?

"Stacey. Stacey." Béa put her hand over mine. "It's OK not to know what to do with this. I didn't either. Professionally, where does this put me? *Je n'sais pas. Je n'sais pas!* It feels as if you can't give someone a pill to make them feel, oh, happy-happy. But: *boff*. You can. It's almost boring."

"Will he move back?" asked Marissa. "To London?"

"I think he needs to be in France for now," Béa said, rapping her skull with her fist. "To heal. To heal completely."

After a silence, Marissa diverted the conversation, asking Béa something technical about the light fitting.

I went to the living room, pretending that the sign-off on my project had arrived. Secretly I'd thought that it had been me who had provoked Gaël's happiness: our new bond; the re-lit sex. Why hadn't he told me? Was he embarrassed? Ashamed? And now I'd found out from his mother, of all people.

Above the concrete fireplace there were photographs of my daughters. It was weird to see them here—as if I'd walked into the house of a stranger. But there they were: one at a Paris water park; another with Gaël in a pine forest. He looked happy. Of course he did.

Marissa's ringtone sounded and there was laughter from the kitchen. Perhaps Patty was OK; perhaps she hadn't died.

I made sure they were still chatting then followed the hall to Béa's former consultancy room. It was a place that had always been off-limits to the girls. Now, it was Gaël's bedroom. Though the door was open, I stood on its threshold, feeling like I too should not go in. The curtains were unopened and the room was dim. His bed was made, and I could smell his scent. I wondered if it was strange to sleep in a room where there had been so much disclosed pain.

As I turned to go I noticed a paperback on the bedside table. I flipped it over, curious, and saw the title was in Spanish. A wave of dread made me feel cold. Gaël did not speak Spanish. I opened the book to a folded-down page. Gaël did not mark his page like this. He hated that I did.

I went back to the kitchen. Marissa was a little pink from the wine, and she stopped laughing abruptly.

"Does Gaël have a girlfriend?" I said.

Béa pressed her lips together. The silence that followed was very tense. "Yes," Béa said finally.

"What's her name?"

Béa didn't look like she would answer me, but then she said, "Isabella."

She cleared her throat. "Now you can sort it between yourselves. It is none of my business." Her voice had become transactional, and I wondered if this was the same voice she used to tell her clients that the time was up. I knew, then, that she had wanted me to know. That's why she had invited us back here. To show that he had not just escaped himself, but me as well.

At the vet's I checked Gaël's Instagram but it only showed meals and skylines. I scrolled through his followers and there she was at the end: Isabella Colas. She was an interiors consultant from Seville, and had an open account. Finding a picture of them on her feed wasn't difficult because it was the only one not of antique furniture. He wasn't tagged. There was a love heart emoji below it, the one with wings, next to Béa's nickname for him: Gigi. Isabella had small eyes set apart.

I felt Marissa's eyes on the picture as we waited for Patty to wake up.

Slowly I put my phone away because I felt as if I might bite into it. But soon there was a loud arpeggiating sound, and I realized it was me, and that, finally, I was crying.

"All this time I assumed he was coming back to us, *he was with her?* And what the fuck, now he's medicated, he's *Houdini*?"

I'd excused his escape because I thought he was in pain. But this was lousy, offensive. I'd never thought of him as a liar.

Before I knew it I was double-tapping the photo, watching the heart icon bang below it. Then I went full crazy and liked all of Isabella's posts until at some point her phone must have buzzed with so many notifications that, wherever she was in Paris, striding the boulevards, she must have recognized my name and blocked me.

Marissa switched my phone off. "I'm sorry," she said. "But I'm not sorry that you've lost *him*. I mean, come on. He was always such a downer. Handsome, but Christ! Oh," she put on her accent despite the fact we were actually in France with actual French people, "'I'm so *sad*. Ah, my heart, my pain!'" Well, children make you sad! They can't help it. It's not their fault. You get through it. They turn into darlings eventually—then you can't *bear* the idea they'll ever leave. Do you think Sancho didn't want to leave? Do you think *I* didn't want to leave? We *all* want to leave. No one *wants* to stay. But they're the grand love affair, in the end. The kids. No one else."

"We were sleeping together again."

"Oh, Stacey," she said, waving her fingers as if she'd just trapped them in a door. "Ouch, ouch, ouch."

We sat for a while. The green walls made me think of pistachio ice cream. "Well, here we are," said Marissa, in her French accent again. "'Two women without their men.'"

"Oh, don't," I said. "I can't bear her."

I thought of the mother-and-child statue in London, and the way the statue always wept, and I thought how I had never really wept for the end of us, because I hadn't ever really believed it was the end. But now Gaël's long lie had broken my own pattern: I take him back, I take him back, I take him back. I too was A/A/A/A/.

My pattern was patience.

Also a scream.

AAAA!!!

The receptionist called Marissa over. There were several papers to sign, then she put her credit card into the terminal. She waited, eyes fixed on the machine, waiting for it to reject her, but the transaction went through without a glitch.

"You know you have to get the will witnessed," I said, as she sat next to me. I could feel the relief coming off her. "You have to sign it, and the lawyer has to witness it. So it's not official. Not yet."

"Oh," Marissa said warmly. "Is that right? Good. Good. Sancho will be happy. I'll tell him. All is not lost. All is not lost."

A little later the vet emerged from the double doors. He wore a mask and hat, but even with the hat I could see he was bald. "Madame?"

Seeing my red eyes he directed the words at me.

In the operating theater Patty wore two eyepatches and purred. "It was beautiful," he said. "But tiny tubes in there, eh! *Minuscule!*"

Marissa rubbed behind Patty's ear, and it twitched with her touch. "I'm so glad," Marissa said, her voice golden. "Oh, I'm so happy."

"*Ne pleurez pas, Madame.* Don't cry," he said to me. Without warning, he squeezed my hand, and I thought how all of the people online were right—his hands really were so soft and gentle. "Soon, she will wake up."

Peek-a-Boo

One evening in July, when I couldn't sleep—the baby was pressing hard on my bladder—I received a call from Carin Mollare. She apologized for the late hour, but said Daddy and his girlfriend were refusing to vacate the Riccione apartment. "We've paid for week twenty-five and twenty-six. I showed him the documents, but still he refuses to move." She said he had added an extra lock to the door.

Carin and I had been friendly during holidays at the timeshare, though we hadn't spoken in a while. "But you always have the ground floor flat," I said.

"We upgraded," she said. "Post-lockdown treat."

I asked her if the management company couldn't sort it out.

"They've moved to Montenegro," Carin said. "No one has the number." She said they'd had to find a hotel, and that her husband was angry. "Will you speak to your Papa? I think he listens most to you."

I called Daddy, but he didn't pick up. I considered what to do, then rang Box. "Daddy's barricaded himself in the timeshare," I said.

"Oh," she said. "What does that mean?"

"The new people can't get in. It's Carin and Egil."

I knew Egil to be a big man, adversarial, and I didn't want Daddy getting into a fight. If I could persuade Box to fly out with me, together we might be able to get him out of there. But, in regard to Daddy—and his almost twice-yearly "incidents"—Box had certain rules of nonintervention; she'd not been to Riccione in years. However, she'd also endured two lock-downs in her gardenless flat, and might be desperate for a change of scene. "Maybe we could go together? Take a trip? Get him out? Can you still fly?"

Box was a little ahead of me, about thirty-four weeks.

"What can we do?" she said. "Two pregnant twins. Break down the door?"

"Carin has paid for the penthouse. We can persuade him to make a dignified exit. We have to stop the situation exploding."

Box sighed. Often she pretended things that happened with Daddy weren't a big deal, or she'd say something like *Forget about him. He's a lost cause.* "What about work?" she asked. "Doesn't Milo need you?"

As Milo's personal assistant I was basically at his beck and call, but he'd been more courteous recently because of my pregnancy, and because of the delayed start to his new movie. "It's just a few days."

"Oh, fine!" Box said eventually.

"Perfect. We can fly out tomorrow and come back Saturday." I scrolled through the airline's website finding us seats. "The Rimini flight's at ten-ten," I told her. "Ancona's earlier. Don't get confused."

"I'm coming back on Saturday, Ani," Box warned. "With or without you."

Daddy loved being in Riccione. He said it was where he felt his best, but it was also, inevitably, where things went wrong. I often wondered if he was killing himself out there, in a trashy paradise, like Nicolas Cage in *Leaving Las Vegas*. Maybe I was being overdramatic, but after the lockdowns it was impossible not to view the world through a hyper-deathy filter. Though it was July, the viral creep was still everywhere in London. People walked around grateful to be through the worst of it, but also empty-headed; a quarter zombie. For the most part, I felt a little numb.

As we flew the plane smelled of warmed ciabatta and liquid cheese. Though it wasn't yet noon, vodka and scratch cards were offered in half-hour hosannas from the loudspeaker. The pandemic meant there were few passengers, which encouraged a hen party—who wore very little, despite the cold recirculating air—to even louder volumes.

I searched for the bride and found her eventually: she was wearing two springy penises on a headband, which made me think of my dream the previous night. It seemed as if all my dreams recently were sexy but also menacing. I'd asked my midwife about this—why the nighttime was now such a relentless sexshow. She'd looked embarrassed and said something about gravid blood flow, the genitals.

Box had a magazine open on her lap: two American actors were photographed in tiny swimming things in Mauritius. "Look at her eyelashes," Box said, peering at the inset. "They're incredible."

"Mink."

"I keep wondering how actors dealt with lockdown. Wouldn't anonymity be painful for them?"

"They're all in therapy," I said. "All of Milo's friends had a blow-out crisis."

"And Milo?"

"Milo found lockdown 'a chance to regroup,'" I said, lying. "One of those."

Box rearranged her position but she still looked uncomfortable. It was funny that she had a much bigger bump because I was so used to us looking identical. Invariably, our twin pregnancies invited gaffes. Around us, people forgot the dark matter of spermatozoa, as if our babies had been conceived via autosuggestion. Were we having twins? Will the babies be twins? Will the babies be identical? I understood the need to find something fairytale in us, something mythological, especially after the horror show of this year. And our chloasma—a mask of pigmentation caused by our janky hormones—made us look even stranger.

Box looked out of the window. The plane flew through cloud and the light on her face flickered and settled. "I was shocked when I saw Daddy in hospital. He looked so bad."

It was rare for my sister to talk like this.

"He's very sick," I said, though we did not really know how sick he was, or how sick he might get. He had once described the pain as *residential,* but you never knew, with Daddy, whether the pain was psychic or physical.

I wondered whether Riccione was the place he wanted to die or the place where he felt most alive. Sometimes I imagined what I might be like on the other side of Daddy's death, but I always came up short, since I could not imagine who I would be without him. But what frightened me most was that sometimes, in the anticipation of grief, I imagined that I might also be free.

"Have you told him we're coming?" Box asked.

"Not yet."

"Is Martine there?"

Martine was Daddy's new girlfriend. "Yep."

"What's the master plan?"

"We lure him out with a free hotel room. A bar tab. A spa day. Two fresh new babies. I don't know. Whatever it takes."

Tumbling laughter came from the hen party up front. A steward had stopped to cheer them on in a drinking game.

"Do you really think you can do it?"

"Sure," I said. I had once persuaded Milo to fly out for a press interview in LA and return for an evening show the following day at the Donmar. "It's my forte."

"And how's that working out for you?" Box said, with surprising bitterness.

I let this rest. The only thing we ever fought about was Daddy. We always disagreed on the way to handle him. I'd believed for a long time in the dumb idea that love would eventually triumph, and that he would come back to us. Box, on the other hand, thought I should threaten him with abandonment, then follow through. I knew she was probably right, but I didn't have the energy for an intervention. I always went when he needed me.

Box put the magazine away and chose a hypnobirthing track from her iPhone.

"You really think that's going to work?" I said, suddenly wanting an equalizer, but she had closed her eyes, and was already somewhere deep inside herself.

The plane had quieted. I tried to sleep but it wouldn't come. I thought about Daddy, holed up in the timeshare. A while ago, with a friend's kid, I had watched an episode of *Thomas the Tank Engine* where Henry refuses to move from a tunnel because the rain would damage his bodywork. But even when the rain stops he refuses to come out. This is dangerous: not to work, not to be useful. Passengers try to pull him, try to push him out, and the Fat

Controller threatens and curses. With all options exhausted they brick Henry into the tunnel, finishing the wall below his eyes, so he can forever see the sunshine; the world; the happy trains of Gordon and Thomas—basically cis, non-unionized, white bro trains—zip past, *poop, poop, poop!* "And there he was left," says the voice-over, "for always and always."

I thought of poor Daddy, then looked at my beautiful twin, and held her hand.

In the high blue enameled light the plane began its descent, and Rimini's pixelated rooftops came into view, with the train tracks slashing the city, and the beach dense with umbrellas, and there was the airport, angled for landing, and the luggage in the overhead cabins rattled downward, until the wheels bounced—once, twice—and the baby pushed my organs upward so I felt like I might choke, and the hen party sang, "Here we go, here we go, here we go."

Our hotel was around the corner from the siege. The concierge talked at us for some time (*Gemelle! Incinta?!*) and only handed us our key cards after misting them with disinfectant. Then she followed us to the lift, pumping her hands as if drawing water from a well, crying, *"In bocca al lupo! In bocca al lupo!"*

As we stepped into the elevator we saw about eight thousand identical pregnant women in the endless mirrored space.

Box looked at our reflections. "Where does this end?"

We slept off the early start, and when I woke I thought of Lucca, the baby's dad, who was in fact Italian. His face, recently, had been slipping from specificity. We'd met on an app, and illegally had sleepovers when the prime minister had told us to shack up or split up. Lucca had wanted to be involved with the baby, but I'd fended him off. Other mothers said doing it on my own would be fine, but their expressions told me they were lying.

Box was still asleep in the other bed. I went out to the balcony, where the sunlight picked out the velvet heads of the geraniums. Motorbikes streamed by, and other people rode city bikes to the beach, where North African men sold things from portable displays. People wore masks and kept their distance, but summer had broken here, deep as a ravine.

The heat was beautiful; almost penetrative. I closed my eyes, feeling its pressure on my eyelids. It felt as if I'd come through an accident.

My phone pinged. Milo was selling his old flat in King's Cross, and the buyers were making last-minute demands. "So the buyers want insurance against the leaseholders not taking out insurance," he said, picking up my call.

"What does that mean," I said, "insurance against the insurers?"

"I don't know. Can you find out?" A Vespa zinged by. "Where are you?"

"Kilburn," I lied. "I'll look into it."

Box told me to be quiet, and I shut the sliding door.

"Was that Mary-Kate?" he said; his go-to joke. He had once set up a dinner in Mayfair with me and Box and the Olsen twins, which hadn't quite worked, atmospherically.

I rang off and emailed his solicitors to reabsorb the insurers' cost elsewhere. The image I used for myself with Milo was that I was a cave, and that when he spoke into me I would echo back his words: a metaphor that had seen me through five years as his PA. But since Daddy got sick I'd been experiencing unexpected rage toward Milo. I was frightened by these new feelings, since going anywhere near expressing them meant I'd lose my job, and Milo was already dreading the arrival of the baby. Milo was also always asking about Lucca, as if Lucca was some great mystery I was intentionally keeping from him. It was an odd relationship to have with a boss: sometimes friendship, sometimes family, mostly servant.

The baby rolled, its skull pushing out of me. I gave it a stroke then pushed it back in. If the boy was a little early, he'd be a Virgo, just like his cousin: genetically speaking, in some mind-bending way, his half sibling.

A WhatsApp appeared from Daddy: "Have you heard of Red Velvet?"

"The cake?"

"They're a K-pop group." He sent a YouTube link for a song called "Peek-a-Boo"; the thumbnail was a group of sexy Korean women. "You've got to watch it," he wrote. "They're really something." I already knew Daddy would have watched the video on repeat. In his retirement—he'd been a civil engineer before his untimely exit—he often became obsessed with odd things: eBay, Aldi, K-pop.

"Daddy, we're in Riccione. Box and me."

It said "Daddy is typing" then it went back to "Online."

"Carin Mollare said you won't leave the apartment," I continued. "Daddy. They're angry. They've paid for the penthouse. They've had to book a hotel."

I waited for the two blue ticks, but they didn't change from gray.

Box came out onto the balcony in a tight black dress with a cup of coffee.

"You look pretty," I said.

"Thanks, babes." She made a kissing noise. "God, I hate this place." Box closed her eyes, as if she were trying to control something.

"Thanks for coming," I said. "I know you didn't want to."

"I'll help you once. Then I'm done. Then I'm at the beach. Understand?"

"Yes," I said, "OK."

I opened Daddy's link and we watched "Peek-a-Boo." The video was intensely adrenal: five Korean women scheming to kill an American pizza-delivery boy while executing a series of brilliant dance moves, rotating a spyglass around their eyes.

Afterward, Box threw the last of her coffee in the planter. "Daddy's so weird." She angled her chair to the sun. We were probably making our chloasma worse, but then, in pregnancy terms, from a certain point everything seemed to get worse—nothing got better.

"That heat. It's *magic,* isn't it?" said Box.

"A potion."

*

Daddy's timeshare was in a modern building, with a ten-by-ten billboard of a footballer in a Barcelona strip advertising Cheetos. The lift was tiny, and Box and I couldn't fit in with our stomachs, so we took the stairs.

At the top, out of breath, we listened to music leaking from the apartment. After a few bars I recognized it as the song Daddy had sent me.

I knocked. "Daddy, it's us!"

I didn't know whether he'd seen my text.

A shadow passed over the door's peephole. "It's me, girls," said Martine. "Let me get your father." Martine—who was always dolled up, even over breakfast—wore sexy nightwear around us, slips and camisoles, saying she felt more like our sister than my dad's girlfriend. Box and I both disliked her intensely.

"Boxy! How big you are!" came our father's voice from behind the door. "And you too, Ani. Oh, it's good to see you girls."

I could tell he was in a high stage of his drunkenness. At this point he would come across as charming—people would want to give him things and make him happy—but soon he would slide out of reach.

I said we had come to get him out of the flat; that Carin had paid for week twenty-five.

"Nonsense! I paid for week twenty-five."

"Daddy? Will you let us in?"

"I'm sorry, girls, but they might be in the stairwell as we speak."

Box opened the stairwell door. "There's no one there."

"It's a trap. They've been here three times today. I've had to fix a draw bolt."

I saw Box doing her hypnobirthing breathing.

"*Cos'è tutto questo rumore?!*" came a woman's voice from behind the opposite door.

"*Scusi signora!*" my dad shouted.

"What is happening?" said Box quietly, looking at me. "Are we in a farce?"

"Two minutes. Please."

"*Le mie figlie sono qui da Londra!*" my dad shouted.

"*Quindi lasciali entrare dentro, buffone!*"

"I can't do this," Box said. She kissed me, but I saw she was scared. "I'll be at the beach."

My head was whirling as I watched her leave.

"Boxy is angry with me," Daddy said.

"Yeah," I said, feeling suddenly sad and disappointed. "Daddy, if you come out you can have the room next to ours. The hotel's empty. A little holiday, all together, before the babies come."

"I just can't," he said, which were the same words

he had used when I had told him at the hospital that he had to stop drinking.

Under the doorway, a folded twenty-euro note appeared. "Why don't you get yourself a gelato, Ani? You must be tired." The K-pop song stopped and restarted. "Martine's learning the dance. It's hard, eh? You work up a sweat just watching it. Those girls are so talented. Did you watch it?"

"I watched it," I said, hearing the zero-ness in my voice.

"Peek-a-boo," he said, and I saw the light blink at the spyhole, and I thought of the game played with little children: the one where the adult disappears.

When we were fifteen, and after our parents had separated, Daddy made our house into the party house. Box and I had always been popular—Scandinavian, monozygotic—but that stock rose when our newly divorced dad let our friends drink and smoke at home, often joining in. At that point he was a smoker, and there were always bricks of duty-free Italian cigarettes to break into, and beers in the fridge, which boys could just go ahead and take. Several of my friends lost their virginity in our attic room. On Sundays, there were bodies everywhere; Daddy charring the bacon in a pan; a pitcher of

Bloody Mary on the kitchen table, as new kids joined the hourless breakfast, half naked and hungry.

The thing Daddy never remembered was that his drinking had preceded the divorce. He always misremembered the story, as if all the trouble started there, and was, in some way, attributable.

I remember wanting all the partying to stop and yet I couldn't let it. Our friends loved our house. I guess it was manipulative of Daddy—a stitch-up—but then no one really understands toxicity while they're in it, especially not a child. Later, pleading exams, Box stopped her weekend visits and stayed with our mother. I continued, though. I'd worked out that if I pretended my feelings could not be hurt by his bad behavior, then it could almost be true.

Over the next few days, Daddy refused to let us in. He said it was an ambush; that if he opened the door Carin and her husband would push their way through. "I know you two are friends," he shouted to me. "I know whose side you are on!" I kept on thinking of Henry, the train, bricked up behind the wall, his eyes tense with anguish. It made me more determined to get Daddy out.

Carin texted me, reminding me her travel insurance had paid for the hotel only till Saturday.

Box had said she would spend her time down at the beach, but her rules, her boundaries—they just didn't hold in this level of disintegration; this level of mess. Each morning she came with me to the apartment. We talked to Daddy through the door, talked to him as if he were a man in a coma.

We said: "This is your last chance." (Me.) "Aren't you running out of booze?" (Box.) "I will do the dance routine. I've learned it. I could do it with Martine." (Surprisingly: Box.) "I think I'm having the baby early." (Me.) "If you don't let me in," (Me) "I will never come back to Riccione."

Nothing.

I had solved worse problems for Daddy, but previously he had cooperated, or submitted, like a baby. Now there was just us and the door, and the door itself—now shut; now draw-bolted—became terrible in its significance.

"I am the door," Daddy said at one point, as if he were Jesus Christ himself.

I texted Carin asking her for more time. She declined. I asked for a meeting. She didn't want to do that either. "Look," she wrote, "Egil's calling the police on Saturday. I've put him off until then. I'm sorry, Ani, I know your dad has some problems."

*

Each time Daddy didn't open the door, Box and I would go down to the fountain at the foot of his block, biting at ice creams from the *gelateria*. One day, as we watched the water tangle, a beach-seller approached us, showing us sunglasses, necklaces, and trinkets.

"Where are you from?" he said.

"London," Box said. "And you?"

"Angola," he said. "A bad year for you."

"Yup," Box said, "very bad."

I bought two pairs of sunglasses and a letter opener for Daddy. It was pretty, engraved with roses, and the only thing that would slide under his door. It was a reliable strategy: gifts had worked in the past.

The seller took my money then faced my palms to the sky. The gesture felt tender, as if I should also open my mouth and receive a wafer. Instead, he gave me two squirts of hand sanitizer. The already evaporating gel smelled of alcohol and the spring passed. "Good luck with your babies."

"You too," I said.

Box put on her sunglasses.

"Don't cry," he said to her.

"Sure." She ate some more ice cream. "OK."

We watched him walk away.

"Oh," Box said, as the tears fell below the dark lenses. "This is too hard."

And yet, despite all this, it also felt impossible not to relax. The heat was a tonic. So was the sea. There was something of the sanatorium to Riccione; as if we had come for a cure after years of plague. We ate a whole heap of shellfish we weren't allowed, and the pickled seafood made the corners of our mouths ache. Our tans made our chloasma look less weird. I slept deeply, and the dreams were still lustful, but without the sadistic tremor of the ones from home. We spent the mornings with the door, but the afternoons were ours.

I could see by degrees how Box too was working off the year. Watching people in the restaurants, in bars, you could see them visibly unload the year's dull violence.

At all costs during lockdown, I'd kept going. I had not stopped for emotion. A few weeks ago I'd randomly walked into St. Paul's at Evensong, and at the end I realized nearly everyone—apart from me—was crying; grieving whoever it was they had lost.

Work people—industry contacts of Milo, people I had never met in person—talked to me of their anxieties and depressions. Everyone regularly started a conversation with how depressed they were, feeling emboldened, I guess, by the national mood. I couldn't stop Milo's actor friends in LA and New York confessing their breakdowns, their divorces, their despair—after last summer—at their newly discovered racism. And yet, not long ago, these people had seemed the most tough, the most implacable. "Ani's so serene," they told Milo. "So tranquil." And I took this as an endorsement, and continued to coast, even to prosper; despite Daddy's hospitalization, the fatigue of the pregnancy, the constant cave energy needed to keep Milo happy.

But over the past few days—perhaps the heat had some truth serum—I'd begun to think maybe I'd carried my quarter zombie with me for a long time: longer than the lockdowns; longer than I knew.

On our last day I woke after a strange dream. It had been sexual, like the others, but this time, immensely pleasurable. There was a stickiness between my legs and I wondered for a moment whether my waters had broken early. I mopped it up with some tissue, and though the dream hadn't been about him, I thought of Lucca.

It hung over me: the question of Lucca's participation, and I wondered why the prospect of him being involved was so frightening. Being Italian, he couldn't understand my rejection. A baby was meant to have two parents, right? His parents in Puglia thought I was mad. Lucca wanted to move in, wanted to set us up before the baby came, and Box too was keen for this. A willing father, who I liked, and who wanted to be involved, who would resist this? Who!

"Let's get married," Lucca had said. "Let's have one of those weddings where the priest has to pray for children and the bride is bigger than a house."

Lucca was nice, like this. Funny, and genuine.

But every time I thought of Lucca a veil of something descended, and I couldn't conceptualize him as anything but another person I would eventually have to care for. Milo, Daddy, the new baby boy: that already felt enough.

I checked my phone. Daddy had texted me a picture of him and Martine on the balcony. She was a slim childlike thing with dark hair and big eyes. Only a little jaundice was left around his hairline. Really, a lot of the time he got away with the worst parts of his behavior because he was just a randy Norwegian with a crystalline blaze in his ice-blue eyes.

*

I went over to Daddy's that morning to deliver the gift. As I was walking I passed a newspaper kiosk and caught Milo on the cover of a tabloid. The photograph showed him drinking coffee in what looked like Soho, wearing the tracksuit pants that—I knew he knew this—nicely showed the outline of his junk. The headline said Milo Reynolds was having a crisis of nerves.

I'd lied to Box when I said Milo had been fine. Late one night in April—Milo had called me away from Daddy's hospital bed—he told me he didn't know who he was; that who he was had disintegrated. He had sobbed in my arms, but inside I had felt only contempt. Really, it felt as if I might detonate. My dad might be dying, I thought, and here I am, with this man-child. I shushed Milo, murmured reassuring things, and made an extra appointment with his therapist.

I got to the fountain by Daddy's apartment and rang Milo, because the tabloids sometimes knew things that I did not.

"I'm looking at the King's Cross leasehold," Milo said excitedly, in lieu of a hello. "The buyers are right! You know what the pandemic has taught me? Insure yourself. Insure yourself to the hilt! Tell them I'll pay it," said Milo. "Tell them I salute their caution."

"You want me to say you salute their caution?"

"Yes," Milo said. "Why not?"

"*Masquerina,*" a passing policeman said.

I replaced my mask and told Milo I'd do whatever was needed.

"Are you all right?" Milo said. "You don't sound like you."

For a moment I thought about telling him everything—Daddy, the door, the threat of the police tomorrow—then shelved the idea.

"Where are you?"

Really, it felt as if something was fusing inside of me. "I don't know," I said, then, surprising even myself, I pressed the red button to end the call.

Later Daddy texted and asked if we could meet at the Lobster that night. "Don't tell Carin!" he'd written, with the sunglasses emoji, which was the one he most overused. This was progress, I thought. I'd slipped the letter opener under his door after the call with Milo. The gift had done its job. We'd meet him at the Lobster. He'd stay at our hotel. He'd be on the flight with us tomorrow. My talents had worked.

When Box and I got to the club that evening the host did "*Gemelle? Incinta!*" etcetera then led us to a table. "No walking. No standing. No dancing. No Coronavirus, OK?!"

We took off our masks and each ordered a glass of wine. The Lobster was on the beach, an empty dance floor at its center, with wicker and leather booths around its edges. Even this early the sex vibe was off the chain: post-viral, euphoric; men in skinny jeans, women in neoprene; hookups on the pristine banquettes.

The setting sun had turned the clouds into roses, and the sea, which from the plane had looked almost limitless, was now foreshortened, its foam leaving its script upon the beach.

"It's like Noah's Ark!" said Box.

"People need a release, I guess," I said, surveying the deep sex-land of the club.

I saw that the hen party from the flight was also here. The bride wore a sash and a diamante tiara. I gave her a wave, but she didn't see me. From somewhere I could smell tomato, geranium.

The wine tasted delicious, so cold and crisp. From our table I could see Daddy's balcony, and in the sky a single contrail. I imagined our flight tomorrow. Martine would be there too. I'd text Carin: "All done! All sorted!"—and someone would tell me what a good job I'd done.

"You know," Box said, "it's not Daddy I'm actually concerned about. It's you."

I didn't want her to be negative just before he arrived. I felt tired, suddenly, and a little separate. At the hen party table I saw the man with shaggy brown hair had joined the bride. He looked like the footballer in the advertisement outside the timeshare.

"Do you remember," Box said, "when we were little, we were eight or nine—it was Christmas, we were still in Clapham. And Daddy insisted on giving me my present first, which made no sense, since we always got presents at exactly the same time. Anyway, when I unwrapped it, it was the satchel with the strawberries on it: the one you'd wanted, not me. Do you remember?"

I remembered this clearly. Box took another drink of her wine.

"And Mummy pulled Daddy away, explaining the mistake. But it hadn't been a mistake. He'd done it on purpose. Switched the gifts. Why would he do that? Why would he play around with you like that?"

"I don't know."

I wished she would stop talking.

Over on the other table the bride was laughing. Inside her mouth was very dark. It looked like she and the footballer would end up in bed tonight.

"It was an accident," I said.

"No, Ani. That's what I'm saying. It wasn't. And the weird thing was you weren't even upset. You knew it was a test. And you thought you could win by not reacting."

I looked again at Daddy's balcony. Someone was up there. Martine maybe. The beach trembled, as if with an earthquake, but it was an ambulance on the road. Aromatics of vaped camomile and jasmine surrounded us in a haze.

"He's not coming," said Box. "He was never coming."

My phone pinged. I thought it would be Milo, reprimanding me for hanging up, but instead it was a picture message from Daddy: a photo of the letter opener. "What am I meant to do with this?" he'd written. "Kill myself?"

I clicked the phone off, but Box had already seen it.

"He's persecuting you," she said.

I put my phone on the table and stared at it for a while. I tried, one last time, to run through Daddy's options, so that he wouldn't be beaten by Egil, or end up in a jail cell, or dead. I imagined the solution, a tiny thing coming out of its hole, then disappearing immediately. Peek-a-boo! Peek-a-boo!

"I think it's time to give up," I heard Box say. "This isn't a game, Ani, it's abuse."

But I knew if I gave up now I would have to give him up for ever.

"I do understand, Box," I said, holding the stem of my glass. "I do understand this is toxic."

"It's just—"

"Please don't say you have your baby now to consider."

"Soon he will do this all over again."

There was a flash of white satin in my peripheral vision; the bride and the footballer were walking to the beach, her name chanted by the hens. I had a sudden memory of when I was a child, hidden in our garden, hearing Daddy's voice calling me. "Ani!" he'd shouted, from far away. "Ani, Ani! Come back, little bird!"

As I finished my wine the song changed. Screams came from the other booths. Women pulled men to their feet as the song riffed through the opening notes, and the stage filled with dancers. It was Daddy's song. I didn't know K-pop had made it over here.

A solitary bouncer tried to disperse them. "*Coronaviroos!*" he said. "*Coronaviroos!*"

But everyone ignored him. They held their masks

in the air like white flags. Then the hens began to do the same moves I'd seen in Daddy's video: rotating a spyglass, flicking their ankles and hips. They were all in sequence, exactly in time.

The crowd parted as the bride came back. She spotted me and Box at the table. "Twins!" she said, taking our hands, pulling us toward the dance floor.

Box refused, but I let the bride lead me toward the hens. I joined in as best I could—rotating the spyglass, flicking my hips. I felt something inside me again, like this morning's arousal, except this time it was festive, and bigger, and my mind felt free, and tranquil. I thought how happy I was to be among these women who needed nothing from me. The bride looked very beautiful in her satin costume. "That's it. You're doing it right," she said, not letting go of my hand, and then kissing me on the lips, as if we were the ones getting married. "Peek-a-boo," she said, "peek-a-boo."

Wedding Day

My ex Nick was getting married to a woman called Esther. Esther wanted our daughter, Paola, to be a bridesmaid at their wedding, and at first I had refused. Nick hadn't been much of a dad; that he should suddenly want his daughter for the ceremony struck me as a little rich.

I asked him if Esther didn't have a niece.

Only Paola would do, he insisted. I supposed Esther had some fantasy about them looking like a family.

Eventually I agreed, on one condition: that he would leave his own wedding and deliver Paola back for her bedtime. Of course, Nick said that my deal was wrong, that Esther would be angry and hurt, but I didn't care. In my life, I had always been a good woman, controlling what it was that I wanted. But recently, I had started to notice my bad energy, and I began to follow it, wondering where it would take me.

Nick had asked me to drop Paola at the church that morning, and we were a little late. Paola sat on the bus next to me in a nest of taffeta and satin.

The bus slowed. The street was all taped up, and in the cordoned area men in white hazmat suits crawled on the road like babies. It looked as if there had been a shooting.

"What are they doing?" Paola asked.

The bus shifted its hydraulics.

"Looking for evidence."

"What?"

"They're looking for evidence," I said louder. It was the mask. "Bits of clothes, things like that. To show who did it."

"Who did what?"

"Who hurt the person."

Paola frowned and I realized I hadn't told her that someone had been hurt. Paola was five. I was unsure how much information she needed. I always got confused about how much reality to give her about me and Nick too. I wanted to be honest, but I also didn't want her to know certain things. Daddy left, just after you were born? Eventually I would have to tell her.

Paola held on to Rabbit tightly, looking out at the examined area. Rabbit was soft and gray. He'd been much chewed.

I had only recently understood that having a child felt like being in a long and dependable love affair. Despite how much I'd given up, which was certifiably a whole life, I'd turned into a worshipful mother. My ex-colleagues in particular found this perplexing; that I would quit my professional life for the unsure promise of a child.

It is not very interesting to be in love with your child; it's commonplace, this sacrificial love, and yet whenever I thought of Paola I thought about my heart; how all my feelings for her were in that tender, silken, sewn-up pocket. O, my heart!

A hazmat grasped a scrunchie from the gutter with what looked like a litter-picker and placed it in a Ziploc bag. He lobbed it to another man, who caught it in his glove. Behind the visor I saw the other man smile.

A long time ago, when I was a child, my aunt by marriage had been murdered by a man she'd never met. She was a glamorous woman with dyed blonde hair and toned arms. She always smelled of toast, which I understood when I was older to be the smell of tanning lotion: buttery and rich, like something about to burn. The detectives told my uncle how uncommon her killing was, how unlucky. Anyway, the uncle soon remarried.

The bus pulled away and we left the scene.

Outside the church, Nick looked nervous. He was smart in his coattails, a corsage pinned to his lapel. Behind them was a hired Routemaster to take them to the reception in Peckham, though there'd only be thirty guests—Covid rules. The destination of the bus was "Just Married."

"Thanks for dropping her," Nick said.

Leonard appeared wearing a navy suit that had a high white shine. Leonard was Nick's uncle, but he'd become my friend when it turned out he had an interest in my academic field. We often had lunch in the guise of talking about semiotics, cultural studies, but soon we ranged over other things. These lunches were always in very expensive places, and I always let him pay. Friends thought it was odd we still saw each other after my split from Nick: an ex-girlfriend and an older uncle. I could see what it looked like from the outside, and from the inside, of course, I saw too the erotic haze in our conversations. I never knew whether I continued because it was fun to anger Nick, or because of the pull to see Leonard.

"See you at eight," I said to Nick.

Leonard took me aside. The way he stood so close made me look for his wife. "Don't do this," he said. I had told him my plan at our last lunch. "You can't make the groom leave his wedding day."

"It's up to Nick."

"That's not true," said Leonard. "It's up to you."

I felt Nick's eyes on us. He'd never liked our friendship, even from the beginning.

"So *you* bring her home," I said to Leonard.

No way Nick would allow this. There was no way I couldn't win; Nick or Leonard—either one would be a victory.

I said goodbye to Paola. Her bridesmaid skirts felt rough against my arms, and I kissed her passionately, as if we were the ones getting married. There was a rush of feeling, a tear, an opening. I caught a streak of white beyond the velvet grass, and wondered if it was Esther, arriving in her bridal gown, the light curious, shedding like the light from a bone, but it was just another woman in a pale summer dress, passing by the church.

*

The bus home took me back through the crime scene. I read what had happened in a free paper: a man had shot a teenage girl from a car window; they didn't know if it was mistaken identity; what. The hazmats were still there and more police had arrived. If the girl had been white (peppy, ordinary grades, hair scraped back) there would have been an outcry, but there was only this paragraph deep in the free paper. As we moved off I watched the burning city membrane, the intimate boundary; white hipster bars, black grocers, Muslim butchers, and south London suddenly seemed the most segregated place in the world.

Paola and I lived in a two-bed on the arterial road leading into the city; host to ambulances and freight trucks from Dover. In the flat, the traffic noise was oceanic, but I was happy here. Upstairs lived Elizabeth, an ancient woman who'd banged a broom on her floor whenever Paola cried as a baby (colic, reflux; each health visitor had said something new). In March the ambulances going to King's had been crazy; thirty an hour sometimes, and Elizabeth had thumped her broom then too, as if I was also responsible for all this excess morbidity.

I wondered what to do now that I was home. Amber, my childminder, who had sleeve tattoos and pink hair and also many thoughts about how I should live my life, had told me I should spend the wedding day with friends, but I'd said I'd do it alone. I had the notion that I had to see it through by myself, and that by the end of the day, I might somehow be transformed.

For months now I'd woken thinking how Nick was finally leaving me. Esther was a safe choice, Nick had told me as much: she was a successful person, owned her own house, her friends were all the same from university. I did not feel challenged by her, but in the nights and early mornings, before Paola climbed into bed with me, I felt bereaved. I knew that after today Nick would be gone in a way that could not be changed.

By now the confetti would be dirty on the road, and Esther would be his wife. They'd be on the bus heading to the reception venue a few streets from here: an artist's studio, a connection of Nick's. I texted Sadie, Leonard's wife, asking for a photo. A selfie arrived of her and Leonard, the shot taken from above, so that they looked thinner than they were. They were a striking couple. Leonard was a tall man, handsome, bald, his wealth almost professionally concealed.

His wardrobe only slyly exhibited its expense—his shirts, his immaculate shoes, the invisible brace he wore behind his lower teeth.

Leonard had said Esther, who worked in PR, was smart. He told me she had the highest grades in her graduate class at business school. I don't know how he knew all that. I don't know why he was telling me. I think he wanted to wound me.

I bore no ill will against Esther. Esther was fine.

Maybe a little trashy, I'd said to my mother after I'd first met her, and taken in Esther's straightened hair, her long nails. I felt no guilt about my deal with Nick. After all, she had him. She had, eventually, won.

It would take ten minutes to drop Paola here this evening, but I knew already Nick would not have pre-warned his wife. He was not a brave man. He would spring it on her at ten to eight. Too bad, I thought. Too bad if I imposed some conditions on his life. And too bad if he didn't like them.

I cleared away Paola's toys and tidied her bedroom. I threw out some drawings and put the good ones in a file. I thought about cooking but wasn't in the mood. I felt a sly energy. I studied my reflection, wondering what I was planning. Maybe Nick would avoid the argument with Esther and as a last resort send Leonard back with Paola after all. Whenever Leonard's colleagues saw us together they gave us inquisitive looks. They were skeptical, he said, when he volunteered I was his nephew's girlfriend. He didn't drop his gaze when he said this: as if to say, what else could they be imagining?

With nothing else to do I got into bed. I used my vibrator and had a powerful climax, then dozed off with it still inside me. When I woke the sun had gone and the light in the room was pale blue.

I ran a bath. In the mirror, before the steam took the picture, I looked at myself again. I wondered if I was a bad person. Leonard had said as much. *Don't be a bitch,* he'd said, at our last lunch.

I imagined Nick returning to the flat with a slice of cake or a bag of sugared almonds. Maybe—the old alliance—we'd laugh at the overdone flowers; the endless sentimental speeches; the expense of the poor catering. We would laugh at all the trouble Esther had gone to; how much everything had cost. He would tell me how much he still hated weddings.

Nick and I had not been married. I can't remember if one of us had been reluctant and the other had followed suit, or whether we'd both been ambivalent. We had always endured our friends' weddings with something like canned restlessness, though sometimes we were moved, and one of us would take the other's hand, thinking unsatirically of what our love might mean, like this. I'd been thinking about it a lot recently: about whose decision it was not to marry, and how maybe it had been a mistake.

In the bath I used the expensive products I kept out of Paola's reach: the ingredients baroque—fig, vetiver, bay. The water was so hot it left a pink reef on my skin.

We had slipped up only once since Nick had been with Esther. I thought of that time: rough, kinky, his hand smothering my mouth. After that, we only ever met up with Paola outside.

Perhaps this was Esther's condition: only ever outside.

I changed into my favorite jeans, and cut the tags from a white T-shirt that gave off a wacky light. I texted Leonard for a picture of the bride and groom. Three dots appeared then went. I didn't know who I was making more crazy—Leonard, or Nick, or myself.

When Nick told me he was getting married, I said Esther would want her own babies. It was a warning shot, fired in the dark.

*

I took a walk, went past Paola's school. Because of the virus, she'd spent the majority of her first year at home with me. It was a Catholic school and there was a huge sculpture of Christ on the façade. On the gates was the school motto: *Ora et Labora*. Paola liked to run these words together on the walk home along the polluted route: *ora, labora, gregora, sheshora*. *"Fedora,"* she'd said, stopping, "hey, isn't that a word?"

I told her it was a hat.

I turned onto the high street, still feeling a little anxious about being outside. People wore their masks under their noses and their chins. I picked up some coffee beans. The roaster or barista or whatever had a long red beard, dense freckles, a working man's apron; he wore no mask. He tried to talk to me, and I was confused about what he wanted. There is a wedding, I wanted to say, a wedding I could not stop!

He asked me—Brazilian? Ethiopian?

He watched me sorrowfully, as if I was failing at something.

Outside, a missing-person poster was cable-tied to a lamppost; a woman with curly blond hair, bad skin, cracked-out teeth. The poster had been here before lockdown and the ink had dripped under the laminate. Opposite was a new restaurant where rich white people ate.

I stopped at the nail salon to kill some time. I often came here with Paola because she liked hanging out on the sofas with the other kids. Sometimes I let her get her nails done too: rainbow colors.

A Vietnamese woman in a black mask waved me over. I'd had her before. She was a tall woman with large ears she usually hid behind her hair. She organized the payment beforehand. "Where's your girl?"

I told her Paola was at her dad's wedding. As she filed my nails I realized I'd come here so I could talk, and was pleased she had questions. Who was Esther? How had they met? Why had we not been married?

"Silly!" she said, making me think of Amber. "Not to marry him!" She applied the polish in quick strokes. "Do you like her? This woman?"

"I don't know anything about her."

Nick had told me in a moment of indiscretion that Esther was not much interested in sex. Too sensitive, he said. I took this to mean she found it painful. How would that work, with him, knowing what he liked?

Looking out at the lamppost, I said, "Did they ever find that girl?"

"What girl?"

I gestured, but she didn't answer.

"Do you have a boyfriend?" I asked, I don't know why.

"What?"

It was the mask, again. "Do you have a boyfriend?"

"I'm married," she said, wiggling her ring finger. The large diamonds were arranged in a pirouette. She rested my hands under the dryer. The fumes were giving me a headache.

I told her we'd been together for six years and that Nick had left four months after our daughter was born. I knew I was delaying her—that she wanted to go to another customer, but I carried on talking. "But that's nothing," I said. "Some friends of ours were together for twenty years, and the guy left six weeks after their twins."

"Oh," she said. "Why would he do that?"

"He has the option? Honestly, I don't know."

Once my nails were dry, I left. Outside, the air had a pre-storm mugginess. The breath behind my mask felt like a hand over my mouth, and I thought again of Nick.

Through the window I saw the manicurist texting on her phone. All these people thought I was crazy. Amber, Leonard, my mother too. Why had I not made Nick settle down, had my own wedding day? And yet I'd sworn, as a child, that I would never be married.

When I got home I ate something. I brushed my teeth, changed my underwear, drank a coffee, put away the vibrator. A friend texted me, checking in. "Keeping busy," I wrote back. Still no reply from Leonard.

"You have to drop this deal," Leonard had said, at our last lunch. I found it amusing that Leonard was fretting over a point of moral principle, when as a corporate lawyer he'd told me his approach was aggressive, sometimes consciously destructive. "Let me drop off Paola on Saturday."

"No," I said. "Nick wouldn't let you." This was the closest I'd come to acknowledging our relationship, and Leonard blushed. The dynamics had changed between us after Nick and I split, and now I couldn't remember if there'd always been this erotic charge.

The way he paid without asking me always made me feel as if I was being taken care of. Outside the curved window there was still no one around Broadgate Circle. I liked London like this: so empty.

"It will cause problems with him and Esther."

"Then they should get another bridesmaid."

"Don't be a bitch," Leonard said. He had never spoken to me like this. "It will look very bad. People will talk."

"Let them," I said, enjoying the clarity of my voice. "I don't care."

Finally the doorbell went. As I buzzed them in I watched from the door. The communal light was broken, and for a moment I couldn't see who was carrying Paola. Leonard? Nick? My heart skipped. I didn't know what would happen with either of them. I watched them turn the corner of the stairs, and saw that it was Nick.

He said nothing as he kicked off his shoes and carried Paola to her bedroom. Rabbit dangled from a hand. I wondered what Paola had seen; what she would tell me tomorrow; how much detail I might get from her.

"Can I have a glass of water?" Nick said. "She's heavier than I remembered."

I poured two glasses of water, wondering if I should have something stronger. I realized I had not expected him; in my heart I thought he would break the promise. I hadn't really thought beyond this point.

"Thank you," he said, taking the glass. Nick sat at

the table, and I saw he was relieved. I wondered if he was glad to be out of the wedding. A smell of cooked food came off him; there was a splash of red wine on his shirt. It was weird to be inside the flat again: together after all this time.

"You're married."

"Yes."

"Was it as bad as we imagined?"

He looked annoyed with me.

"I'm joking!" I said. "Congratulations." I offered him a toast. "To the bride and groom."

We were lit for a few seconds in the disco of a passing ambulance.

"Did the bride look marvelous?"

"Come on," he said. His voice warned me off, but then he smiled.

It was then that I realized he was happy, and the pain of this felt acute, and precise, and beyond how much I could possibly hurt him.

"What did you do all day?"

Amber would have told me to lie, but I couldn't find anything to say. "I thought about your wedding."

"What about it?"

"I don't know."

He waited.

"I was glad for you. Also sad, at some points."

"Well, there you go. Life, isn't it."

"That's it."

We sat there for a while. "How was Esther?"

"Pissed off."

"You hadn't told her?"

"No. I said Paola would go crazy if anyone else took her."

"Did Esther believe you?"

Nick looked at me, looked at my mouth. He reached over and took my hand. "You got your nails done?"

I felt a burning sensation around my jaw, then it spread to my chest. He looked beautiful: I could imagine his chest under the tensed shirt. "Yes." I thought of the salon, and remembered the clean sparkle of the pirouette. "The manicurist told me I was mad not to have married you."

He was still holding my hand.

"And what did you say?"

"That we didn't want to."

He nodded. "That's it," he said, taking his hand away. "That's right."

I held on to my neck. I couldn't look at him. I felt a pulse of dark energy and wondered who I was—this woman; this type of woman. Nick was watching me. Perhaps he was remembering the last time we were here. Even for us, that time had been rougher than usual, marked by violence.

"Why did you make me come back here?"

"I don't know," I said again, though now I knew the lie.

Nick scraped his chair back and walked through to the hall. I followed but didn't switch on the light. It was a narrow space. He bent to tie his shoe, his face level with my hips, and I could see the tender fold of his neck where it had been shaved. I imagined the hands of his barber on his skin. He was making me crazy; I was so alive with desire.

When he stood he took hold of my wrist, quite hard. He was angry with me; I knew that. "I wish I never had to see you again," he said, forcibly whispering into my ear. He leaned his forehead hard against my cheekbone, and put his hand between my legs and almost lifted me up. I heard him say something, but couldn't make out the words.

He let me go, and left.

I stood in the doorway. From the little window I watched him walk through the alley, startling a fox, which ran from the bins. Something wet trickled from my nose. I caught it with my hand—a nose-bleed, the blood dark in my palm. I found a tissue and knocked back my head.

I wondered if I'd got what I wanted: if I'd finished the day as I'd hoped. I stood there for a while, imagining Nick, a little sullied, reentering his wedding; Esther's suspicious, waiting face, and Leonard's envy. As I held my nose there was a strong smell of the varnish on my fingers, and in my mouth I tasted blood, as if I'd just made a kill.

Hurt Feelings

Chalazan dominated the market for over-the-counter painkillers, combining, in various admixtures, paracetamol, ibuprofen, caffeine, and codeine. It had segmented the market into migraines and headaches, joint, menstrual, dental, viral, and child, and now—with Claudia and Mo's new ad campaign—the company was soon launching Nocileve, for chronic pain.

To Claudia, chronic pain looked like the pits. All the patients in the focus groups were gray with fatigue, haunted by the unknown etiology of their illness, worried to the point of terror that their doctor didn't believe them; that in fact most of the medical establishment believed that their pain—lit gas rings under the skin—was phantasmic, psychosocial.

They had no lesions; no injuries. Why did they hurt? So much, and all of the time?

Suzette, the creative director at Cake, had promised that securing Nocileve would bring Chalazan's household cleaning and personal hygiene divisions in-house too. It would be a big steal; very big. Probably there'd be a write-up in *Campaign*.

It would be a boon for Claudia and Mo too. They'd worked as a creative team for seven years now: Claudia as copywriter, Mo as art director. Recently, though, Claudia had begun to suspect Mo was restless. He was ambitious. He found anything that caused career deceleration abhorrent: her pregnancies (there'd been four) actively seemed to wound him. She was currently eight weeks from her due date, and once again it was making him agitated; faintly hostile.

In fact Claudia felt she could no longer trust him. No way could Suzette have such a fine index of her absences without Mo supplying them. Mo had always been hard to pin down as a person. She suspected he hid a great vat of chauvinism behind his lavish personality. His flirtatiousness with both men and women hinted at bisexuality, but at night in the bars on Cowcross Street he'd hoovered up pussy with very little discernment.

In her last full-term pregnancy (hypertension, anemia), Mo had hated her lack of drive. He had wanted them to be poached by a rival agency as leverage against Cake. "Sometimes, Claudia," he'd said, "you just have to slap your dick on the table." She did not know what this meant, or what she was supposed to do with her dick. It felt inevitable that she would become a victim of Mo at the same time that she clung desperately to him. He was Suzette's star, whereas she was heading out alone into the dark hinterland of maternity leave.

This morning, though, he'd bought her a coffee—or at least he'd sent the intern, Rose, to fetch her one. It was nice when Mo was nice to her; it reminded her of how they'd been in the beginning.

"Flat white," said Rose, handing Mo his cup.

Claudia could smell something punchy on Rose's wrists.

"And I got you a one-shot latte? That's what my sister drank when she was pregnant."

"Thanks," said Claudia. When Rose was out of earshot, she whispered: "Wasn't she meant to be our diversity intern?"

"She's South African."

"She's *white*."

Mo shrugged. "The task force interviewed her."

The anti-racism task force was a unit of three white women headed begrudgingly by Suzette.

Over their coffees they watched one of the focus groups. The video began in a medical setting: a doctor explaining, via the ruby lactate on the tomographic map, the neuroinflammatory response of M.E. patients.

"I always thought it was made up," said Mo, frowning at the video.

Inflammation was the real killer, the doctor said: primed microglia attacking the sufferers after minor events, like a quick call with a friend; then an oversensitive sickness response causing an autoimmune cascade into IBS, headache, psychomotor slowing, sleep disturbance, anhedonia. "The need to offer relief for idiopathic pain," the doctor continued, no doubt primed by Chalazan's R+D guys, "is currently a need unmet."

"I didn't know what was wrong with me," said a man called Glenn, a spokesperson supplied by CIPS, the advocacy group for Chronic Inflammatory Pain Sufferers. "I got home from work one day and just crawled into bed. The next morning I was swollen, head to foot. They tested me for everything, but found nothing," he said. "Then they sent me to a psychiatrist. Nothing. I only got the diagnosis after they'd ruled everything else out. It was so depressing. 'What's caused it?' my friends asked. 'Why now?' My husband became my carer. I was used to having so much energy, then, *wham*, it was like being hit by a car. And you know what really sucks? If I overdo it only a little—go to the movies, say, where I literally just sit in a chair—I'm immediately triggered. I'll be exhausted. I'll be totally punished the next day."

"Gah," said Mo. "It's so grim."

Nocileve wasn't in any way different from other over-the-counter analgesics, but Chalazan had identified a big proportion of the market that didn't feel cared for—or catered for—and that was the important thing. Mo and Claudia had one week to come up with the campaign before Suzette moved it to another team. This was how Suzette worked: she played the teams against each other.

"It's the unending nature of it," Glenn continued. "It's hard to have hope. My doctor said we should do the McGill questionnaire, then he got frustrated, because none of their words were accurate. Let's just try the McGill words to describe the pain. 'Cramping?' he asked. 'Pulsing? Is the pain pulsing? Does it throb? Sear? Maybe it sears?' I said it gnawed, it was heavy, I said I dreamt about it; he said I was being too lyrical. Eventually, he threw it out. The McGill thing. He said watching an episode of *Frasier* can take his mind off a long day. The next time he asked me to make my pain into an animal. I called it a fox. I said, this fox stinks, it stinks like hell. Like its fur has been rubbed down with used cooking oil. And it lies across me in the mornings. My doctor got excited about the fox, he said it would help, but it hasn't. It just makes me hate it more. The worst thing is it's pointless. The pain stops me from living. Sometimes I just want to die."

After her first labor with Sylvie, Claudia had come to think of herself as an aristocrat of pain. The experience had thinned the membrane between life and death, since there was no way she wasn't being poleaxed—vaginally, prismatically—by the force of the baby sucking out her insides as it emerged, vividly purple, smelling of sea-soaked rocks and coated in vernix surf. But she'd only had to go through that for seven hours, and the pain had at least been productive. Nothing like Glenn's misery in its sheer ongoingness. He was right, though: pain, in its essence, was pre-language—which was why, during the contractions, all she'd been able to do was low, like a cow stuck in a swamp.

Claudia had been clear with Barbra, her midwife, that this time around it would be an epidural and season four of *Succession*. Why should she suffer? And why should Glenn, with his soiled fox, after a trip to the shops? But this week Barbra had scheduled an appointment with Dr. Lim, Claudia's obstetric consultant. Barbra had never done this before, and Claudia understood it to be medically significant, because midwives never really wanted to involve doctors if they could avoid it. What would she do, if Dr. Lim wanted her to stop work? Work took away all bad feelings.

"In the end the doctor thought I was crazy," said Glenn. "He couldn't understand me. He just wanted me to leave him alone. In fact, he was the one who looked depressed. There was this haunted look in his eyes, when I came into the surgery, as if he hated me." Glenn paused. Maybe he was looking at the cameraman. Maybe he was seeing the wreck of his world. "I am sorry for the doctor. I am. But what I am looking for is a way ou—"

Mo paused the video. "Vron"—Mo's girlfriend, a dental hygienist—"sometimes brings home Novocaine. You snort it and go spacey *for hours*. I might be addicted?"

"How are you two?" Claudia asked. Vron had

moved in with Mo over the summer, though they'd only met on New Year's Eve. She had the most impossible hair, so thick and curly, it was inches wide.

"Yeah, good," said Mo, who was always costive about his girlfriends. "How's Joe?"

"Fine," she shot back, though she didn't really know how her husband was, since they both spent all their time working, or looking after Sylvie, and Joe was obsessed with his new diet and going to the gym, and neither of them spent any time talking about the painful things that were so obviously hurting them both.

Claudia stared at the O of Glenn's mouth. "I think it's about despair." She flicked in the dossier to *Pain Asymbolia*. "Did you read this case study? These people feel no pain. And yet their pain centers still light up when the doctor sticks a nail in their foot, or whatever. How can that be?"

Mo drained his takeaway cup, shrugging. Mo's talent was somehow contiguous with laziness: he wouldn't have read any of the studies; he let her do that.

"But do you know what *doesn't* light up?" Claudia persisted. "Their emotional centers. People with pain asymbolia are failing to make *emotional* meaning of their pain, and therefore feel nothing physical."

"So what?" said Mo, looking at her, deeply bored, just as the doctor would have looked at Glenn.

"So if you give someone paracetamol, it can actually lessen their emotional pain too, which then makes the physical pain less meaningful. Look at this guy"—they both turned to the frozen wasteland of Glenn's man-of-sorrows stare—"he's *spiraling* into despair."

"Maybe he needs an antidepressant?"

"True. But that's not the point."

"What is?"

"The point is we have to sell him a painkiller."

At this she remembered to take her own mini aspirin. Seventy-five milligrams, every day, for her hypertensive heart. Perhaps the aspirin was creaming off some of her own affective stance—certainly she had blank moments for seconds, which turned out to be minutes, hours. A few weeks ago Barbra had shown her, with some displeasure, how Claudia's diastolic numbers had left the green and entered the red of the diagrammatic rainbow. "This is where you don't want to be," Barbra had said. "You want to be way, way down there. *In England's green and pleasant land,*" Barbra sang tunelessly. Why was her midwife singing "Jerusalem" at her? Anyway, Barbra said, looking intently at Claudia's laptop bag: any higher, and things would have to change.

Claudia started the blood pressure machine and opened the app. Mo too woke his phone. Every day he witnessed the escalating atmospherics of her blood pressure, but he never commented on the procedure, nor did he ask her how she was feeling. Maybe he didn't want to pry, or maybe he was just an arsehole.

As her hand drained of blood, Claudia watched Suzette instead. They had a catch-up tomorrow. Claudia dreaded these meetings: it seemed impossible to predict Suzette's variable moods of ice and jazzy warmth. Anyway, they had such an air of an HR commandment it was almost impossible to feel anything authentic.

The cuff let out its air, and Mo too let out a regretful sigh. Claudia's phone gave a mournful bleep: 148/95. Way too high. Way, way too high. What would Dr. Lim say, with a reading that bad?

"Are you done?" Mo said, then unpaused the video.

"—Out of this pain!" said Glenn, who then dissolved into tears as his face was replaced by the revolving Chalazan logo.

*

Barbra had looked surprised by Claudia's answers to the booking-in questionnaire. First, there was her hypertension. No one medical ever thought Claudia would be hypertensive: she was slim, and didn't look the type. Then, there was the depression, which, she had to admit, still hadn't gone away, and which continued to wake her in the mornings, painful contrails of terrible dreams, until she could get into work and forget about it all. Finally, there were the stark numerals on the form, which had made Barbra pause: Gravida 4; Parity 2.

As Claudia's blood pressure rose she'd seen more and more of Barbra, a faintly erratic New Zealander with fluffy hair and pink Crocs. Barbra was often telling her to take it easy and to concentrate on the baby—as if Barbra herself suspected that Claudia's devotion to work had led to the miscarriages. Claudia didn't even know what this meant: concentrate on the baby? Barbra wanted her blood pressure to come down, so of course she would say this. "What are you so tense about?"

Work, Claudia wanted to say, but couldn't: work! Aside from Joe and her daughter, Sylvie, who was increasingly like a French New Wave beauty, work was all she consciously cared about, but she couldn't admit this to Barbra, who anyway didn't really want the Rolodex of all her lively miseries. Suzette was on her case; Mo was being weird. Claudia just wanted to get through her last few weeks at Cake without pissing everyone off with her shonky heart, protein-rich urine, and appointments with Dr. Lim, a cheerful but candid woman from Kuala Lumpur who kept on saying, "It's too high! Why's it so high? You're not even fat!"

The next day Claudia reviewed past campaigns for analgesic ads in the Cake archives. "I take Advil because my kids deserve a mom without a headache," read one, showing a woman cowering before a wrecking ball. "Get back to normal, whatever your normal is," read another, under an older man driving a golf club.

Shame was a big part of it. That's what the ads implied: that there was something shameful about chronic pain, something whiny, but also something non-chronic and fixable. (Was it the interns, who did this work, ripping out magazine ads, and filing them away?)

Last week a spokeswoman from CIPS had briefed them on the public awareness campaign that would precede their web and TV ads. CIPS, via three quarters of a million pounds of Chalazan seed funding, was planning the campaign for chronic pain in November. This would widen the net for Nocileve's customer base, expanding it from the terrible daily baseline, of, say, Glenn, to people with persistent niggles: sore stomachs, aching insteps, the cold.

CIPS had also agreed to supply patient-experts in what was now labeled Pain Awareness Week (PAW) as well as advocate Nocileve to their members. This optimized market would then be perfectly conditioned for the ad campaign in the run-up to Christmas, to catch sufferers at their most depressed. Claudia knew, in her over-industrious heart, that this was the type of behind-the-scenes shit that always made a campaign fly. It made advertising look easy. The bell pull; the bell; profit's ding-dong . . .

Claudia wondered about using Glenn in the TV ad, but Glenn was a total downer, and probably couldn't act his pain even when electrified by it. All of yesterday Mo had gently parked her ideas, a strategy she knew he had learned recently at mediation training. Recently Mo had been going to more and more evening workshops and networking drinks while she was doing Sylvie's bedtime. Who had he met? And what did he want from them? Claudia could attend networking events in the day, but they were only ever attended by middle-weight mothers her own age, so what was the point?

It was not impossible, she thought, that Mo was going to ditch the partnership system altogether, and go solo. Copy was increasingly undervalued: it was all about the image—you could see that in the graduates coming from Wycombe and Watford—portfolios of beautiful pictures, and not a word, not one, between the pages. If Mo left her, where would she go? And what would she be? Returning back to work from maternity leave, totally alone?

"Hi, Claudia," Suzette said, later that afternoon, pronouncing it with an "ow" like a Mitteleuropean. She beckoned her inside. "How are you? How's lovely Joe?"

Suzette found it hilarious that Claudia was married to a primary school teacher at a state school. Claudia began talking, but Suzette's phone rang, and as soon as she answered it she began an argument with Accounts. "No," Suzette barked into the phone. "Release early, iterate often. It's not fucking rocket science."

Suzette wore sleeveless black dresses even in winter, and her thinness suggested something glass-like.

At lunch she was known to eat only several heads of broccoli. She had a tan from a February trip to a Caribbean island she wouldn't disclose: something double-barreled, Turks and Caicos, or an acronym; the BVIs. Suzette always took a complicated way of flying there because she refused to travel with the carrier whose account she'd lost in her twenties at MKR. No one was allowed to ever mention the airline's name.

To their one, Suzette had four D.A.D. Pencil awards. Her campaigns had been extraordinary—for Whiskas, NEFF, Honda, NatWest—increasing market share for her accounts by double points. Claudia had once aspired to be like Suzette. Now, Claudia tried to avoid her, at all costs.

Suzette put down the phone just as the baby did a weird slithering thing against Claudia's abdomen. "Wow. It really moves like that," Suzette said.

Claudia put her arms over her stomach. "Have you sorted the parental return-to-work checklist?"

"Paternal . . . ?"

"Parental."

"Sure. Yes, I mean, it doesn't exist right *now*. But it will, when you come back. For sure. I'll check with Rose," said Suzette. "She's pretty good, don't you think?"

Claudia shrugged.

"How's Chalazan?"

"Interesting."

"Tell me," said Suzette, and Claudia saw the light change in her gaze, quick as a wing, which signaled true interest.

"The mood of the focus groups was really heavy. Like, despair? Despair that nothing will change. Or that the future will be worse than the present. Their pain is almost world-breaking."

Claudia thought of the pain of Gravida 3. So stupid, she thought, to have named the baby, to have invested it with a whole life.

"It's emotional, too," Claudia said. "They *hate* their pain. It slows them down. Did you see that campaign—'Count your cholesterol, or end up in the morgue'?"

"Didn't they get into trouble for that?"

"Yes. But trouble is good," said Claudia, "trouble is free. Fear is a huge driver in consumer choice, isn't it?"

"When's the pitch?" asked Suzette.

Suzette definitely already knew this.

"Eighteen March," Claudia said.

Suzette paged through her diary. "So the thing with Jasper is he'll want continuity."

Claudia suspected Suzette and Jasper—Chalazan's COO—had once been fucking, which was how Suzette had secured the pitch in the first place.

"They'll be jumpy after Biderdorf," said Suzette. "Above all they'll want continuity from pitch to launch. You could sit out this one presentation, but be involved behind the scenes as much as you want. You can then rejoin when you're back. Do you have a date for that yet?"

"You can't keep asking me that. It's against the law."

Suzette palmed her head into her hand like a tennis ball prepped for serve. "So many things to remember!"

"Where does this leave me?"

"It's up to you."

"You've just told me it would upset the client if I was there and then wasn't there."

"I know: aren't they sensitive? But it's *entirely* up to you." Suzette flexed her hands in a funny little prayer: "You're the Holy See. It's that corporate desire to *completionize*. To have everything operate like *clockwork*." As she said this she turned the four pencil statuettes a half-turn each. "Anyway it might just be too much stress. You know. What with your heart."

Claudia sometimes wondered, in these moments of abject sisterhood, what Jacinda Ardern would do, but she was honestly too tired, with her cardiac load and unborn baby, to channel Jacinda. Barbra often talked about Jacinda. Maybe most New Zealanders did.

Suzette resumed: "I'd hate to think you're putting your body through this unnecessarily. Your health matters most. You see, advertising's like a magnet: all the atoms have to face in the same direction." She pushed together her balled hands then sprang them apart. "Otherwise? No magnetism."

She adjusted the family photographs on her desk. It was always surprising to Claudia that Suzette wasn't just this entire thing, that there were descendants; daughters. "What do you think of Vron?" asked Suzette.

"Mo's Vron? She seems nice. Less desperate than the others."

"*Tant pis,*" said Suzette. Claudia didn't know what this meant. "I always think he's a bit sparkier when he's single."

Maybe Suzette wanted to fuck Mo? Was that it?

"Are you going for lunch with them on Sunday? We've been invited. Bruno's coming too." Suzette didn't wait for an answer, and Claudia wondered if this was another of Mo's moves: invite Suzette; ignore Claudia. "By the way, I want you to be on my anti-racism task force."

"Doesn't the task force need continuity?"

"No."

"Doesn't the task force need a person of color?"

Suzette's cold green eyes swept the office floor. "Does it *look* like we have rich pickings?"

The way Suzette's hand hovered over the overworked mouse meant Claudia knew she had been dismissed. As she was leaving she saw a new picture of the cosmos on the office door. A supernova. It was kind of cheesy, for a woman like Suzette. "What's this?"

"Oh," said Suzette, looking up. "That's the heat death of the universe. I look at it when I need reassurance." And then—really? Claudia wasn't sure—but she thought she heard Suzette murmur *ba-boom, ba-boom, ba-boom,* like the metronome of a heart.

Later, Claudia read the Insight. She read the data, then reread it. It was unlike Mo not to have more ideas. Perhaps he was storing them so that he could be the hero who saved the day at the eleventh hour. He'd done that before. She felt sorry for all the people she'd read about. She'd been in her cloud of psychic pain for two years, but they'd been laboring in theirs for decades.

Suzette walked past, heading to Anna and Ayman's office. They were working on a campaign for a mobile phone company, and their ideas so far had been rejected. She could see Suzette's blonde bob but none of her face. Though Claudia couldn't hear anything, she knew Suzette would be talking in her new Batman voice. After Roberto had left, this was now how Suzette told people off. Roberto had been the only Black creative at the agency, and Suzette had made his life a misery. It was no different to how she treated everyone else, apart from, of course, it was, since she could have tried, just a little, to be nicer to him. After Roberto had gone, HR had told Suzette she had to stop shouting at people; hence the new Batman whisper, which might be worse.

As punishment for Roberto, and because Suzette had single-handedly ruined their diversity stats, HR had made her lead the anti-racism task force. But Claudia knew her boss still called people "fucktards," that she kept a pillow in her office to scream into, and that the toilets were still called crying cubicles by the nearly all-white staff.

Mo didn't seem to mind Suzette's personality. But then Mo wanted everything to be pure Don

Draper—she could see it in the way he treated Suzette, Claudia, even Rose; offering his patronage then withdrawing it without notice. The other day he'd offered Rose a training session in a graphics app, but when she turned up, he dismissed her and went back to throwing a ball against the wall.

Claudia had had boyfriends like that.

"How did the catch-up go?" asked Mo.

"Oh, fine," said Claudia. "Suzette told me my health was really important." She wouldn't tell Mo her position on Nocileve was threatened; she wouldn't give him that pleasure. "Are you having lunch with Suzette on Sunday?"

"Oh, Vron's organized that. Do you want to come? You'd have to get a babysitter."

"Sure," she said, wrong-footing him. "We'd love to."

"I'm cooking," said Mo. "A leg of lamb, studded with garlic."

"Sounds delicious."

Joe hated her work engagements, which was fair enough, given how her colleagues either ignored or belittled him. She wondered if, when they got a babysitter, they could steal an hour together before the lunch. But what would she say? She knew Joe was suffering, but she knew also that she couldn't touch it. Fountains of pain; nowhere for it to go. Now, they existed almost entirely separately.

"Do you have anything?" Mo said to her.

Claudia looked away as Anna strode toward the toilets. "No." She took a swig of her iron water. It tasted of blood. "Do you?"

"I heard a rumor," he said, "that Suzette is a Romanian countess. Apparently we shouldn't refer to her as Your Highness but Your Serenity."

There were only three days left for the campaign, but Wednesday was kiboshed by meetings with Barbra and Dr. Lim. Barbra was not the problem. Barbra was quick, efficient; it was Dr. Lim who was in demand; who trailed after her, like jet oil, waiting times of hours and hours.

Claudia sat in the waiting room alone. Joe couldn't be here for all the scans, because—although he could, legally—he also just couldn't with his school timetable. Many women were alone here anyway, so it wasn't a big deal. They were surrounded by posters urging them to eat well, exercise, not drink coffee, not sleep on their backs, not smoke (but vape if they had to?), and absolutely, 100 percent, try to breastfeed. Claudia scanned the small print to see which advocacy groups had sponsored the campaigns: MaTs; BBys; CaFaS, but the letters meant nothing to her.

She made notes on her phone and rang Mo for a catch-up, but he seemed annoyed by the interruptions of the medical loudspeaker, and parked her taglines with his new mediation thing ("Can we look at it from this angle?"). Claudia really didn't want Nocileve transferring teams come Friday. She knew how much pleasure it would give her to see the campaign when she was deep in the midnight zone of motherhood. She would think: I did that. She would think: And I can do it again.

But as she looked around the room she realized the day was almost gone. She thought of the pain inside the hospital; the ability of the staff to do the biggest thing in the world, which was to tranquilize pain. She leaned on this thought, thinking it might inspire her, but got nothing. Instead she remembered coming to this wing after the second miscarriage, at nineteen weeks, for a final "evacuation."

They had already told everyone about the pregnancy. Something so striking about how she felt afterward—inside, a core of pain—but Joe couldn't talk to her. And friends didn't want to talk about it either. Especially now, while she was pregnant. *Look!* She saw it in their eyes. *You already have another, and some people can't have any! Be grateful for what you have!*

But that late baby . . . oh! In her mind's eye she'd given him a face, a name, a life, a future . . . her boy. And sometimes, without warning, the unextracted pain of him could freeze her where she stood.

Finally, Dr. Lim called her through.

Claudia was now familiar with her consultant's candor; the halogen lights of the examination room, the gray-and-white slush-puppy of the ultrasound screen. Claudia was familiar too with the kitchen towel over her legs and the cold KY on her abdomen. At least Dr. Lim was fun. She had no bedside manner, which Claudia appreciated, since everyone else in the medical establishment seemed to ceaselessly infantilize her.

As Dr. Lim moved the wand over Claudia's stomach they engaged in the preeclamptic call-and-response. "Any flashing lights?" ("No.") "Floating specks?" ("No.") "Any headaches?" ("No.") "Pain just below the ribs?" ("No.") "Any swelling? I mean, unusual swelling," she said, passing her gaze over Claudia's feet. "Ignore those marshmallows." ("No.")

The lube smelled slightly spermy, like a linden tree in summer.

"Did you experience hypertension in your last pregnancy?"

Dr. Lim asked her this every time. "Yes."

"A stressed mama, hmmm?" The baby appeared, paddling legs in the amniotic fluid. "You're awake today, baby! Usually you're asleep, Fat-Fat."

Some weeks Claudia had to drink a cold Sprite to wake him; other times, do star-jumps. The scanner swept the baby's face. Claudia saw the baby's profile: the tiny nose, and the lips, which were just like Sylvie's. She felt her heart, normally so folded around the iron staff of Suzette's workplace, unfurl and gladden. That was the crazy thing; these babies—the love she felt for her daughter was extraordinary, maybe even ten times what she felt for Joe. "Hello, baby," said Claudia, happy suddenly. "Hello."

"Any name?"

"Not this time."

Dr. Lim's breath smelled of chewable Gaviscon. They listened to the baby's heartbeat: so fast! Racing away! The fastest it would be in all its lifetime! "OK! Get dressed." Dr. Lim snapped off the acoustics. "And how is your mood?"

This was unexpected; Dr. Lim didn't usually ask her this.

"I mean, this whole thing," Claudia said, as tears

uselessly pricked. "I spend more time here than at work."

"Is work very stressful?"

"I work in advertising."

"Eclampsia," said Dr. Lim, "means lightning." She zigzagged her hand, cutting air from air. "It can strike at any time."

"I know," said Claudia. "I do know that."

"Did you watch *Downton Abbey*? Lady Sybil? Season three? Women died of it: all the time! Nothing but a wooden spoon to chew on. But seriously. You should consider scaling things back." Dr. Lim's voice went weird and sincere. "There's quite a lot at stake."

They had discussed her pregnancy journey in a previous meeting. She couldn't bear the idea that Dr. Lim might bring it up now.

"It's up to you," Dr. Lim said. "But rest now could make things better later on. I could sign you off work if it makes things easier."

Claudia looked at her. "Are we at a . . . critical juncture?"

Dr. Lim tilted her head.

"I mean, do I have to decide now?"

This time, Dr. Lim nodded.

Claudia thought of the pitch, but also of Joe, who probably couldn't endure another loss, and Sylvie. She thought of the new baby's nose in the ultrasound; the tip, upturned, and perfect as a nut.

Both the second and third pregnancies had started miscarrying in the work toilets. She'd only been six weeks with the first, and hadn't felt very much, in terms of emotion. It was funny, she thought, pressing a sanitary pad into her pants before returning home to bed and ibuprofen, that someone else was using a crying cubicle next to her, probably weeping about one of Suzette's put-downs, when a tiny baby, no bigger than a thumbnail, was being slowly junked by her hostile womb. She guessed maybe it was not funny at all. She'd been sad, that time, but not overwhelmed.

That had come with the third, much later. She'd never felt such granite-like pain. She'd fallen in love with her unknown boy, and could not believe she would not get to meet him. In the days, at home, a funeral traversed her brain. And yet there was no one to grieve him with. Joe went back to school. She was off work, but there was nowhere to mourn.

When she returned, Mo had been nice to her.

Maybe he thought he'd been spared another career interruption, though that was a nasty—but not impossible—way to think.

No one talked about it afterward: not at work, not at home. Joe just wanted to eat his cornflakes, gazing at Jean Seberg, and to get on with life—school was stressful. They would have another baby. He took up exercise. Went to the gym. Became obsessed with new diets.

At work Claudia and Mo were put on a campaign to recruit sixteen- to eighteen-year-olds into the Army, targeting certain demographics in the poorest English cities. No other team would take the brief, and Claudia had accepted it, much to Mo's surprise. What did it matter, she thought—as their video ad sent chipper boys and girls to their deaths over netted obstacles into the humid jungle—life offered short rations; make of it what you will.

Sunday lunch had been moved to a fashionable Italian in Clerkenwell. It was dense with advertising people, and the light in here was tented and dim. There was a constant murmur of prosperous sounds.

At the table Joe looked scruffy, especially next to Suzette, whose blowout gave her the look of a

Republican in an attack ad. Next to her, Vron was talking to Suzette's boyfriend, Bruno, and Joe was telling Suzette about his veganism. Suzette pronounced it with the stress on the second syllable: "And when did you turn ve-*gan*?"

Claudia knew Suzette would be bored, and so let Joe carry on.

They'd relocated from Mo's apartment to the restaurant once the get-together had transformed into Claudia's farewell lunch. "Oh good," Suzette had said, when Claudia had presented Dr. Lim's sign-off letter. "Now we get to spend a whole heap of Cake money." And Mo too—though he had hidden it—looked relieved by her early departure. Now, she was out of the way, and he could accelerate as fast as he wanted.

She had done the right thing. She'd taken Dr. Lim's advice. She was acting on Barbra's injunction: concentrate on the baby. Next week she would do nothing. She would simply look after herself; she would lounge. But already, it frightened her. What would she do? Left alone to simply think?

The mains arrived. Joe looked at her beef shin and winced.

Bruno was very good-looking—Suzette's boyfriends always were. He was a tall Argentinian, a competitive body-boarder. Claudia asked him about the difference between his sport and surfing.

The size of the board, he said, was much smaller; plus, different foams. "And, you're prone," he said—shooting a curl off his forehead—"on your stomach." He made a shape with his hand, showing, she guessed, a wave.

"When are you due?" Vron cut across.

"Twenty-four April."

She narrowed her eyes. "A girl?"

"A boy."

Vron looked disappointed.

"I didn't know that," said Suzette doubtfully.

"Yes," said Claudia, with some finality. "A boy." This time, she'd said nothing.

"And how are you feeling?" said Vron.

She considered telling them about the preeclampsia, then shelved it, deciding that she didn't like Vron. She said she was fine.

Bruno began talking about his mother. She had been beset, he said, by a degenerative disease, which was like motor neurone disease, but wasn't. Suzette had obviously told him about Nocileve, forgetting it was mostly phony. For years, he said, his mother was gaslit by doctors. Psychiatrist after psychiatrist saw her. "But nothing is wrong with my mother! Like an ox," he said, tapping Claudia's forehead, "up here."

"That's very common. To assume it's psychosomatic. You know what my mother does? She wears her *worst* clothes to the doctors. And no makeup. Absolutely no makeup. If you look too good you won't be believed. And doubt is a form of poison to these people."

Claudia saw she had cleaned the beef off its shin.

Bruno put a hand on his heart. "I have always believed her. Always."

"She might try an antidepressant."

"I've just told you," Bruno said unhappily, tapping his own forehead this time, "it's not *up* here."

Claudia couldn't be bothered to explain—pain, affect, meaning.

Suzette was talking about a shoot for an Australian beer brand in Tasmania. They were being forced to take the distrusted airline, she told Joe, because there was no other way to Hobart.

"You know they put two million tons of carbon into the atmosphere a *month*?" said Joe.

"I know," Suzette said, wincing. "Appalling. I hate them."

Claudia smiled to herself, thinking how much better Joe was than all of these awful people. He seemed to catch her looking at him, and he smiled at her, uncertainly.

Suzette dinged her glass with her steak knife, which was still streaked with blood. "To Claudia!" she said. "Off on sick leave, poor thing." Suzette made a sad face then brightened up. "And to that little Cake baby in there!"

Everybody raised their glasses. "To Claudia!"

"Bring that baby in to meet his office daddy, won't you?" said Mo.

Joe narrowed his eyes. She smiled. What the fuck did that mean?

"And, of course, 'Hello, happiness!'" said Suzette, toasting once more, and everyone repeated it, including Joe, not knowing he was echoing the new Locileve strapline.

Over tiramisu Vron advised Suzette on other possible routes to Hobart, and Mo was telling Joe about the campaign. It had been at a quarter to four on Friday, he said: dangerously close to the deadline, when it came to them. And of course, it was simple, really, like all good ideas. The ad would show a woman, tunneling through earth toward daylight. When she comes to the surface, she can finally breathe again. "Hello, happiness!" she says. "Hello!"

"It came to *me*," said Claudia. "Not us."

"Of course," said Mo, doing a little bow.

More vividly, though, Claudia remembered what happened afterward. After their pitch in Suzette's office ("I love it. It's perfect."), Claudia had gone to box up her things while Mo stayed behind. Claudia couldn't help watching him across the office floor as he laughed at Suzette's jokes. His artwork was on the whiteboard, and Claudia's strapline was above it.

Hello, happiness. Hello.

But when Rose had brought them coffees, Rose had not left. In fact, Rose had taken Claudia's seat.

In the restaurant, she saw she hadn't touched her dessert, and that Bruno appeared to be talking to her still. "I want to try Mama on something else," Bruno said, with his hand on her forearm. Why was he touching her? "I will send her the Nocileve," he said. "See if it works."

"The Nocileve?" Claudia thought of Glenn's death-mask grimace; his invisible, anguished sepsis. "Yes. Why not? She needs something to believe in." She thought of Rose, who would take her place at the Chalazan presentation. She thought of Barbra, of Dr. Lim. She looked at Joe. She thought of the gone, unmourned baby. "Otherwise, you know, that pain can overwhelm everything."

Flatten the Curve

Anxiety was Deborah's thing. In fact, it was her friend. Back in January, she'd been anxious about the pandemic before anyone else: she'd stockpiled the baby's formula, and amber soaps that smelled strongly of Dettol. And when the pandemic had finally shown up, Deborah had felt a strangely pleasing sense of confirmation:

Hello. Here you are.

I've been waiting for you.

Maybe my whole life.

It turned out the virus was—and had been, as suspected—everywhere: on the baby swing, the button at the traffic lights, on the dog come to slobber moronically over her daughter's pristine hands.

But when the disease arrived her anxiety oddly lessened. She'd read how neurotics actually became less neurotic during the Blitz because the bombing raids only confirmed what they had suspected all along: the world is frightening; the world is bad.

And: I knew I was right about this, all along.

Never before had Deborah felt as if her vision of the world was in alignment with reality. Now she was just like everyone else. Or—ha-ha!—everyone else had the bad luck to be just like her.

That March, Deborah decided to make their house impenetrable. They only left to go into the garden, or, when the kids were really going cuckoo, Cal took them to a nearby school field. They bathed their groceries. Sprayed the post. All their friends were doing this too. Cal had had pneumonia three years ago. Men like him—late forties, fit enough—were dying in ICUs.

Despite the newness, this withdrawal also felt deeply familiar. Deborah was already an expert in declining pleasures. She could diet for months and instead of reintegrating foods she would take more out: no sugar, then no fruit; no carbs, then no alcohol. More than other people, she could deny herself nice things for longer. She found she just never wanted things as much as other people wanted things.

*

One morning Deborah took the children into the garden. She watched the baby as he poured the flowerpots onto the patio. Two lines marked where he'd wet through his nappy. The baby was loutish and oversize; nothing fit. On her phone she googled "How big is a one-year-old?" and clicked on portable children with slim waistlines. She wondered if she was bored. At first she'd been devoted to their internment, but it was weeks since she'd even put her foot outside the front door.

She heard her neighbor open his gate and soon squares of Andrei's chestnut curls were visible through the trellised fence. He and his wife were Brazilian. He was on a work call; Andrei was something in marketing. Before lockdown Deborah had seen Andrei almost dance to avoid a dogshit on their road. He'd looked beautiful, agile.

Deborah carried his body in her mind like a souvenir. Really, she couldn't even remember if she had genuinely found him attractive: maybe she'd made it up, now that her old life had the helpless sexy voodoo of a forgotten dream. Anyway Deborah only ever talked to Andrei from ten feet behind the shared fence, so that his breath could be ventilated away in the breeze.

She wondered if Julia and Andrei ever heard them having sex. Deborah never heard them having sex. Come to think of it, she never heard the neighbors on the other side having sex either. Deborah suspected they had a second home and were swapping between them. She thought lesbians would be more right-on but maybe that was another heteronormative way of thinking. They had hand-drawn pictures of NHS rainbows in the windows, despite the fact they had no children.

"How's things?" Andrei said, after hanging up.

"Oh, you know," Deborah said. "On it goes."

The baby gave her a gummy smile, and Deborah stroked his back. "How's Joey?"

"He's fine. Now he doesn't even ask to go out!"

"Same with Zara."

It had been hard work, at first, separating Joey and Zara. It was like the Montagues and the Capulets! But now the kids just gazed at each other through the windows.

"We could play badminton," Andrei said. "One day, over the fence."

"Yeah," Deborah said, as she traced the arc of the pathogenic shuttlecock. "That'd be nice."

Zara wandered into the garden with her magnifying glass. Lately she'd been pretending to be a spy.

She was wearing a swimsuit, which was dangerous, since the material's ultrasilkiness seemed to make her giddy. She was an embarrassingly sensual child, prone to erotic dancing in her bedroom window, which Joey would sometimes watch from his trampoline. Deborah wanted to tell her six-year-old to stop but didn't know if this would make it worse. "Hi, baby," she said, cupping Zara's chin, resisting the urge to kiss her, since maybe all the kissing was the problem.

Zara held up the magnifying glass. "I can see you," she said. "I can see everything."

Next door the netted walls of the trampoline began to tremble. "Oh," said Zara. "I didn't know Joey was there."

"Zara!" Joey said, his hair mushrooming at the apex of his jump. "ZARA!"

"Do you want a dozen eggs?" Andrei said. "I have several pallets of eggs."

"I'm here! I'm here!" shouted Joey.

"No," Deborah said to Andrei. "Thanks."

"Don't go, Zara! Don't go!"

But Zara giggled and wandered off inside, and the baby pulled a plant from the soil, and Deborah thought of expensive hotels, clean and sexy, without history.

*

The weather that April took on a peculiar LA clarity: nothing but blue enameled skies, endless brightness, hot rooms with little mystery. She sensed Cal was bored too, though he was enduring house arrest better: he'd found an exercise regime, the garden bloomed, he spent more time with the kids. The more he flourished—tonally, physically, spiritually—the more it nettled her.

Deborah worked in contract HR. At the start of lockdown her company had been accommodating of her flexible working request, but recently they had tired of it and had asked her to come back full time. Now, she and Cal swapped work and childcare in a terrible cascade of two-hour shifts. Someone was almost constantly trying to put the baby down for a nap.

She thought she would be able to endure this for months, but already she was beginning to fray. Honestly, she'd had her fill of joy and togetherness, and was done with all that. The problem was the autocycle of cleaning, cooking, and caring. The problem was the lack of change: the next calendarless day, there was still nothing to do, even while the sky burnt, a blue tub.

*

Without a haircut, there was a new density to Cal's beard; he'd started to oil it with clove. He had long hair and dark shamanic eyes. Often people thought he was Arabic. In the sunshine he'd tanned deeply, and his hands had grown rough from gardening. He looked better than ever, but Deborah felt her attraction to him lessen. A friend said she loved lockdown because she and her husband could fuck over their lunch break. Cal and Deborah weren't doing much fucking. But neither were Julia and Andrei, or the lesbians, who'd mysteriously come back.

"Nine hundred and thirty-one people died yesterday," Deborah said, over dinner one night. Every evening she told Cal the daily body count.

Deborah always watched the news, because it gunned her toward the fact that they were doing all this for a moral purpose. When she watched the broadcast bar charts she willed herself to grieve for the dead, but it was hard to hold twenty, thirty, forty thousand people in her mind at once. She imagined the dead in buses, in concert halls, in stadia. She felt bad about this too: she wanted to be more horrified, but the more she tried to conceptualize the dead the bigger the metaphor she had to reach for, and the more impossible they were to imagine.

Deborah looked at her dinner: roast leeks,

cauliflower, rice. She knew, then, that the vegetables just could not rise to what was needed of them.

Cal was vegan. There was little that could be done about that either.

A sound came from the sky. They hadn't heard a plane in a while. They lived in the city, but the city was stricken, subdued. "Do you think the best thing to do is just lie down and take it?"

"Take what?" said Cal.

"Like, stop militating? Be more Buddhist, accept surrender: that wanting things only leads to grief. Etcetera?"

Cal looked at her blankly. "What is it that you want?"

"I don't know," she admitted, though she thought: not this.

They didn't speak for a while as Cal checked WhatsApp. She herself didn't look at her phone at the table. And anyway, she hated WhatsApp. The constant messages made her feel under siege.

"I spoke to Satomi yesterday," Deborah said. "She told her husband: 'Give me the virus! Put it in my veins! I cannot spend another minute with my children!'"

"Isn't Satomi Buddhist?"

"I don't know. She might be."

They carried on eating. They'd used food against the tedium, and now she felt softer, inflated. Deborah looked around the dining room. They'd only just bought their house, and she wondered if it would be renewable, or if it would always remind them of this year's terror and lassitude. She knew they were the lucky ones: a bedroom for each child, a garden, but reminding herself of her luck didn't help raise the shelf of her mood. "All of this. Why doesn't it seem relative? All that shit, I mean"—her voice gathered reverb—"the makeshift morgues, the tiny funerals, why doesn't all *that*"—she gestured to the window—"not make *this* more bearable?"

"This is hard."

"I always thought I was the queen of this. Endurance." She thought it would be the same as quitting cigarettes, sugar, booze. "Turns out, I don't think I am. I'm actually intensely fragile. Weak."

Cal pulled her onto his lap. She touched his beard and its Death-Star blackness. He was so handsome. She loved him, and yet wanted more of him. It seemed like he was going to say more, but the baby cried out, and instead Deborah went to him.

Upstairs she soothed him easily. He didn't fight her, and so nothing of the moment had its usual ambivalence. She kissed him while he slept, kissed him so many times she risked waking him, until she persuaded herself to put him back in the cot.

She peeked around the curtain. The window was open, and she saw Andrei, on a call again, speaking Portuguese. She wondered about the type of woman with whom he would have an affair. He looked up at her and smiled.

She put her finger to her lips.

Andrei made a "mea culpa" gesture, sneaking off to the shed, though she hadn't meant to tell him off.

Downstairs she heard Cal doing the dishes while watching skate videos on his phone; she could hear the flame-like crackle of the opening credits, and then the grind of wheels. Sometimes, in the evenings, all they could do was commune with their phones. They wasted the evenings because they had no energy for them. In the evenings they were done for.

The breeze sucked the blind in and shot the room with light; that must have been what roused the baby. Deborah thought of the time she'd flown fourteen hours, Tokyo to London, and the light from the cabin window had been an endless afternoon. Yes; this drift, this waiting, this negligent eating.

Despite Deborah's crisis in resolve there was still twice the amount of work to do in about half the time. Other companies contracted out their legal policies to Deborah's, and her company advised, in terms of HR, what was legal and what was not: most of it was. She spent her time showing clients how to furlough, how to recoup government money, how to report losses to get Covid grants. Sometimes, it felt rotten. Cal worked as a manager of a water aid charity. Sometimes that made her feel bad too.

During her Zoom today Deborah talked casually to her colleagues about parenthood in a way she knew the other women found offensive: how the baby played with the hair straighteners, the oven, the plugs, but when she heaped on the sourness, the men laughed even more, and she felt like one of them. She didn't know why she did it: why she couldn't report that life with the kids, now that they all operated in a constant perceptual indoors, could also be benign, even delightful.

Downstairs, children roared. Birdcalls zapped from tree to tree.

Her little desk was shoved against the window; their bed was in the background. She feared the children coming in, yet longed for them to interrupt her, so that she might say to her colleagues:

Look! Look!

This is what I'm dealing with!

Her boss arrived and the call moved on. Most of their discussion was about a retail brand: an Asia-Pacific multinational that had been investigated for taking a governmental Covid loan and spending the money on an ad campaign. And if their fraud wasn't yet in poor taste, Deborah thought its slogan, "Click for Calm," which encouraged shoppers to surf out the national crisis via online retail, was almost as bad. Was the alliteration meant to echo "Clap for Carers"? But she kept her opinion to herself. The CEO said it would soon blow over.

Zara wandered into view behind her.

"Oh, hello!" nearly everyone said, apart from the CEO.

"Say hi, Zara."

Zara said nothing and flopped onto the unmade bed, the look in her eyes positively bridal. "I have to go," said Deborah, conscious of Zara's ritzy swimsuit. "Time for homeschool."

"Have fun, Deborah!" someone typed privately in the chat, with a winky face. "I've been learning patisserie!" Then an emoji of a baguette, which was not, she thought, patisserie, but just a baton of bread.

Zara was in fact getting close to no homeschooling.

"Where's your magnifying glass?" Deborah said, closing the laptop. "Aren't you still a spy?"

"Lost it."

"Close your legs, babes." Really, it was rampant; when had this happened? "Are you missing your friends? And school?"

"No."

"Where's Daddy?"

"Doing yoga with the baby. Can we play aliens?" said Zara. "Or mermaids? Or babies?"

Babies was hands-down the worst.

"Flam flark manoosh," Deborah said, as Zara pulled her into her bedroom. "I'm from planet Zog."

They played for half an hour, quite pleasantly, and Zara's face grew joyful as Deborah really committed to her role. Finally, when Zara had grown bored, she climbed onto the windowsill to watch Joey on the trampoline, and banged her palm against the glass: "Joey!"

"Zara!" he said at the height of his bounce, then "ZARA!," again at the top, then "I LOVE YOU!," which made Zara dissolve into hysterics.

Julia was also in the garden, in a terry-cloth dressing gown. Deborah cranked the window to hear if the call was interesting, but knew from Julia's tone that it was her mother, who frequently called from São Paulo.

Deborah looked for Andrei. She sensed he was a

little more decisive than Cal, a little more straightforwardly *masculine*—no yoga, no charity work; just selling people shit, and occasionally doing weights in the garden. She wondered if he was a reflective man. She wondered if he and Julia kept secrets from each other. She was thinking about him more. On a Zoom call his face often rose unbidden in her mind. She noticed that when she thought about him, she felt a tug of something like desire. She thought about him especially at nighttime, when Cal was on his phone, and she was already in bed, and when she did her brain went dark, as if it were filling with water.

A cloud of apple blossom filled the air around Joey, kept aloft by the trampoline's electrostatic. It was so beautiful that for a moment Deborah forgot herself. The suspended snow hovered about him, then, like a magic trick, it showered down, and the image was over.

Deborah started waiting for Andrei in the garden. She couldn't work out if it was Andrei specifically that she desired or whether it was any stranger that might induce in her again the feeling that she lived inside a body.

Andrei had begun to sunbathe topless, or to work outside topless. He seemed to do very little parenting.

Sometimes she heard him and Julia arguing, which reassured her, since she and Cal were arguing too, over the smallest things—things that would have never upset them before—but then neither of them had agreed to be holed up forever in all this starchy proximity.

More time happened. There was a meteor shower, which she somehow missed, and the sky at night was so clear that the stars shone with cold intensity. Satomi had posted her a book on Buddhism that she said was helping her endure lockdown. Deborah tried to bear in mind impermanence, as the book suggested, especially in relation to her own suffering, but it didn't help. She'd thought she was a master of not wanting things, but now all she did was want things she could not have: she wanted to see her friends, she wanted to dance in a club of sweaty bodies with a raging EDM track; and, most of all, she wanted Andrei, who did something weird to her saliva glands.

At work she'd buried the "Click for Calm" campaign by hyping the company's new diversity stats, and the CEO thanked her for it.

The birdsong grew increasingly insane, like a tropical aviary outside her window at four a.m. She began to eat the children's vitamins.

The lesbians had gone again.

Meanwhile the numbers dead were so big it was impossible to visualise, even with metaphors. At eight o'clock on Thursdays she and Cal stood on their doorstep and clapped for carers, though she didn't put in much effort. Her aunt had told her that in China there was a tradition that a citizen should *eat bitterness*—that one just had to endure things, without speaking, without complaining—and above all, without applauding.

Eating bitterness seemed better than clapping. The clapping felt no good. She thought some of these people clapping were probably also willing vectors: people who went out, and socialized, and didn't care about killing others. She thought of the disproportionate number of brown and Black doctors and nurses and porters dying in the NHS, and only reluctantly smashed her hands together, thinking it was altogether too stupid for all this senseless tragedy.

She continued to watch Andrei obsessively in the garden. "*Olà*, Deborah," he'd say to her, as she watched him from the baby's bedroom. When he spoke in Portuguese it turned her on. "*Olà*, Andrei," she'd reply girlishly. She tried seeing into their bathroom. After a nap one day she found herself masturbating, imagining him banging her against the fence that separated their houses, and it was so hot that she came in about a minute.

One evening Deborah cooked a beef bourguignon. She knew it would upset Cal but still did it anyway.

"What are you doing?" he said.

The kitchen smelled of animal fat and boiled red wine.

"The baby only eats mush, you won't eat meat, Zara won't eat flavor, am I the only one who consumes *normal* food?"

He told her she was being crazy, but she could tell he was wounded. He went back to the year's best Vines, and they sat watching the folkloric internet try to wash away their unhappiness.

"What's wrong with you?" he finally said, sprawled on the stained sofa, because they weren't allowed nice things until the baby was older. "Why would you want our kids to eat that? An *animal*? We agreed they'd be vegetarian."

"I'm sorry," she said, wondering what, in fact, was so wrong with her that she'd made their children a meal from the constituent parts of a cow.

"Do you even *care* about climate change?"

"Yes," she said, wildly ashamed. "I care! Of course

I care." On the screen, a man fell off a roof and into a pool. "Maybe I could make you dessert? Out of jackfruit, or something?"

"No. You can't just . . ." Cal looked around the room. "De-leverage."

"I don't know what that means."

Cal looked at her, and she thought he was going to say something long and filmic, but he didn't. "What's wrong, Deborah?"

"I don't know."

"I don't know, I don't know! That's all you ever say. Well, figure it out. I can't live with you like this."

Cal went to bed, and she wondered if she should join him. Maybe if they had sex it would make things better, but she'd probably kiboshed that with the brisket.

As soon as he was upstairs, Deborah drank the rest of the cooking wine, then opened a new bottle. She drank another glass and scrolled a gossip website. For an hour she looked at pictures of the Kardashians, then George and Amal. She wondered if lockdown was an escape for them, since they hated their celebrity, though that too could just be a ruse. She scrolled through Adele's furious weight-loss; then to a story about Grimes and Elon Musk, who'd just named their baby "X Æ A-12." She wondered what those figures signified. Maybe it was a Buddhist chant? Deborah said "X Æ A-12" a few times, wondering if it might help quell her desire for Andrei, which also felt like a sum with no definitive answer.

She put on a coat and went outside in the hope of finding Andrei in his garden. Maybe, with his wife in the house and Cal asleep, they could get into something deep; something lovely, and rare. She could smell weed from their side, but when she stood on the picnic table she saw it was Julia, smoking a joint.

"Hi, Deborah. Wish I could offer you some of this."

"Oh, don't worry. Probably shouldn't."

Julia took a toke. "When was the last time you went out?"

"Like out, out?" said Deborah. "Not sure. Forty, fifty days?"

"That's incredible. We at least go to the supermarket. Or the park."

"Cal had pneumonia. We're just being careful."

"But aren't you going out of your mind?"

"It's like a movie about the Jews in Germany," Deborah found herself saying, and though she herself was Jewish, she felt on shaky ground. "You keep thinking, 'It's 1938! How can you not see the danger? Get out of Berlin! Just get out of there!' And I see old people on our street and I think—'It's 2020! Just stay at home! Just an extra day!' Instead they're out there, in Virusland, hugging their friends like they *want* to die."

Deborah felt ashamed of her Holocaust analogy and sought to row back. She was drunker than she'd realized. "At least, that's what I tell myself," she said. "You know. To keep us going."

"I mean, boredom does weird things to people," said Julia.

Deborah shrugged. "Can't be bored, dead."

Andrei came out of their back door. She realized he had, at some point, turned almost triangular. Such a neat little waist. She wondered if it was a stereotype to think that when he walked he almost sambaed. "*Ciao, amore,*" Andrei said. For a racing moment Deborah thought that was for her. But also: wasn't that Italian, rather than Portuguese? "Hello, Deborah," he said.

"Are you going out?"

"Just the supermarket," he said with a wink.

Julia rolled her eyes. Andrei unlocked the padlocked gate and disappeared down the shared alleyway. "*Adios!*"

Now Spanish?

"He has a poker night at a friend's house," Julia said. "They play cards. Drink whiskey."

"Inside?"

Julia shrugged. "Everyone bends the rules a little." She finished the spliff. "Night, Deborah," she said, and went back inside.

Deborah felt suddenly disgusted. It was as if Andrei had deceived her directly. He was one of *them*: a person willing to kill someone because he couldn't be bothered to stick to the rules. Andrei was killing people. Potentially, anyhow. She thought of her moral internment, her suffering—one of the four noble pillars in Satomi's book—and of all the times she'd ever fantasized about him. She rested her forehead against the gate. Here is your pillar, she said, and she began to hit her head against the fence. *Bang, bang, bang.*

"Wake up, Mama!"

Deborah felt one of her eyelids being opened by her daughter's magnifying glass.

"I'm here," Zara said, "to arrest you."

Deborah sat up, her hangover instant. "Oh, fuck."

"Mummy, don't say that word. The baby's crying."

The bands of Zara's swimsuit sparkled in the dim light.

"Why are you wearing that?"

She looked at her swimsuit. "I wear this every day."

"You do? Why don't you put something else on, sweetie?" Then she changed her mind. "Actually, do what you want."

Deborah went to get the baby. The cot sheets were wet with leaked pee, and he was still wearing the dungarees from yesterday, without a T-shirt, so that he looked like a miniature mechanic. Ultimately, the baby would be bad for her hangover, but right now his solidity prevented her squid-like anxiety from returning completely. It was the booze. The booze always made her way more anxious.

"I'm here," she said, cuddling him. "I'm here," while genuinely feeling as if the sense of who was here might disintegrate at any moment. *Thump, thump* went her head, and she remembered how she had banged it against the post, and then the shock of Andrei's illegal outing; and how much she had drunk, afterward, because her idea of him had been so wrong, and the pain of her disappointment had been so surprising.

Downstairs she put the two empty bottles in the recycling, then retrieved one and put it on the side so Cal would pity her. She made the children pancakes and gave Cal a lie-in so that later she'd have something to trade. She made Zara a heart-shaped pancake, and the baby threw his to the floor.

"Look, Mummy!" Zara said, cutting off its top lobe. "My heart is BROKEN!!!! Do you get it? Huh? Huh?"

"I get it, baby."

When Cal woke she told him she was hung-over. He kissed her and said he'd take the kids out for a long shift. He was so kind; she was so awful.

"Have you forgiven me for the beef?" she said. "I'm sorry. I think I'm going mad inside."

"It's fine. This is weird," he said. "This is all very weird."

When they were gone she went on a bad internet dive. She read how global warming was melting the Arctic permafrost, and when that ice went millions of microbes, which had no intimacy with the human immune system, would be released in vaporous plumes: anthrax, smallpox from the Kolyma River, raging botulisms; who knew what else the ice hid? Then the fish would eat the microbes, and a local hunter would eat the fish, and then the hunter would sleep with his wife, who would serve coffee to the Canadian oil seeker, who would journey home to Toronto, closing his eyes on the suburban train toward home; his breath, real as cloth, billowing like iridescent laundry into the extinct future.

*

Eventually, Cal and the kids came home, and again their bodies, their delightful realness, consoled her. She thought how she had three people to love, and how she would die if anything ever happened to them.

Later, while the baby was napping, and Cal was in the shed, she watched *Frozen* with Zara. She liked this movie. She wondered if she too could harness her anxiety as her superpower, just as Elsa could eject icy shafts of power from her hands. She wasn't sure, though, that her anxiety was anything but a darkness, and one that she could much better live without. Elsa was discovering this for herself, but Deborah was sleepy, and there were long stretches where Princess Anna was kind of annoying. Just as she was dropping off to sleep, Deborah heard the back door slam.

She roused herself, ready to find Cal in the door-way. He would soothe her completely, tell her that he loved her, and that everything would be over soon.

Instead it was Joey. He was smiling at her as if this was all completely normal. She stared at him. The garden gate. Had Andrei forgotten to lock it after the illicit game?

What was Joey doing inside her house?

"Please," she said, her mind feeling sharp, and not at all hung-over. All of their work suddenly ruined, by someone as stupid as Andrei. "Please don't move."

"Hello," Zara said happily. "How did you get in?"

Without warning Joey leapt toward her and they fell together onto the cushions. "You look nice," he said, hugging her tightly.

"Joey! Joey!" came a voice from down the hall. The sound of Andrei's footsteps followed; then, he too emerged in the doorway. The funny thing was that up close, Andrei didn't look like how she had imagined him; not at all. "Joey!" Andrei looked astonished. "Oh, I'm so sorry, Deborah! Joseph, no!"

"Andrei," Deborah said, though she was thinking only of Cal. "Andrei, please get out of here."

Just then sunlight spilled into the room, illuminating Zara and Joey, who were on the floor like Romeo and Juliet entombed—and Deborah saw the dust of the pumped cushions, circulating the room like dander.

Dino Moms

We all just felt so bad when Mrs. Cooper kicked it, though the mystery surrounding her death also made us less attendant to our grief and instead intensively speculative: what was she doing out, after dark? Why hadn't she taken her gun? Was she banging Patrick, was that it? And what would happen to her daughter, little Sandy Cooper—only eleven, and so ill prepared for life by her mother, who'd been so lucklessly chowed by the park's Carnotaurus?

For weeks afterward we wondered what Patrick would do with Sandy. She was increasingly sassy and disruptive, and he'd acted fast with tricky families in past seasons. *Dino Moms* is a scripted reality TV show: think *Jurassic Park* with vets, at a summer camp where we live all year long. It's about "Dr." moms and their "Dr." daughters—and without the mom element, it doesn't really work. But Patrick kept Sandy on. Why, no one knew.

Since Mrs. Cooper "went to get her reward"—as Mrs. Appleton would have it—my daughter, Mol, has been hanging with Sandy more, and when the girls are in the same episode you can add, like, ten or twenty percentage points to the viewing figures. They play well with a younger audience who aspirate upward, and so wherever we go now, Sandy comes too. It's kind of a drag, to be honest. Sandy's often cranky and brings her bag of mournful stones with her everywhere she goes: *clunk, clunk, clunk*.

Luckily Sandy has to at least *sleep* at Mrs. Appleton's cabin, which is good news for me, though no good for Mrs. Appleton, who has spent most of her time on the dinoranch almost totally zoned, and now has to attend to a sorrowful girl who has close to zero self-awareness. Poor Sandy; Mrs. Cooper was no great shakes in the mothering department either, which means Sandy's been lumped with one dud after another.

Since Mrs. Cooper's "departure," Toro (the fans' name for the Carnotaurus) now gets closer to our enclosure. He leaves oversize emojis of poop by the electric fence; in the mornings, aromatics of kerosene suffuse the compound. I ask Mrs. Appleton if she thinks Toro is lonely and wants a mate, since he moans all night; roaring and gnashing.

"Oh no," she says, "I think he just got a taste for us."

Each family takes it in turn to film with Toro, and Mol has become increasingly tetchy about these scenes. Toro has red eyes and a roar like breaking metal; his strings of saliva are as tall as our cabins. I know Mol is frightened but there's little I can do: I show her the tranquilizer darts, the loaded guns, I tell her the turkey farm puts Toro off our scent. It's Sandy who's had this effect on her, but I simply can't give in every time Mol lets her caveman brain get the better of her, and, usually, a little into the Toro sequence, she settles and has fun.

Anyway, coming here has brought us both a lot of joy and a lot of togetherness, and that more than makes up for the dicey parts. My favorite time is lying in bed with Mol, falling into what we call "ranch sleep": a sleep so deep it's dreamless. Soon she'll be too old for all this; possibly she is already. I tell her I love her a bajillion times a day. Maybe it's too much, but my mom never said it to me—even in her last moments, when she too was heading to claim her last reward.

*

Today there's an alert for an injured Ankylosaurus in the Western Pen. An Ankylosaurus is quite a thing: a three-ton dino-hedgehog with bones for quills, and a tail like a medieval mace. Funnily enough the ranch alerts always make me feel apprehensive. My veterinary training was with small domestics, and the dinos' damp and scaly skin often makes me feel sick. Unlike a cat or gerbil or just your plain old Pomeranian, their Cretacean eyes feel inhuman. It's a physical reaction I try to watch and overcome, and usually I'm OK after a few minutes. I say the same thing to Mol whenever Toro is close: watch the fear approach, like a wave. Don't run. Experience it fully. It is in you, but it is not you. When Mol told Patrick she was fearful after what happened to Mrs. Cooper, Patrick bought her an app for meditation, though I'm pretty sure she hasn't used it.

I respond to the alert, saying we'll attend. Patrick's voice responds: "Bring Sandy."

My heart drops.

Dino Moms is a mix of mild threat, veterinary procedure, and brand-sponsored moments. Over the course of the week we film outside sequences and inside sequences. Patrick directs anything that's filmed on the ranch; anything inside—our emotional relationships, mother-and-daughter breakfasts, play-dates—is caught by the home cams, then edited into the show.

Each episode is named after us—"Mrs. Leiss and Mosasaurus," "Mrs. McCabe and the Megalodon," etcetera. That's why we never use our first names with each other. It's a strangeness we maintain off-camera, but then things *are* pretty kooky here: we live with dinos! Our daughters are "doctors"! All our periods are in sync!

Mrs. Appleton lets us out of the compound and into the ranch. Sandy and Mol are in the back of the Jeep, though I can't hear their chatter over the engine. The desert is red; boulders rear, big as cruise ships, and the scrub looks like algae on a rusted sea. I love this place. I feel happy here: closer, I think, than I've ever been to who I want to be.

The camera crew are setting up when we arrive so I give them a few moments. This scene will be core to whatever story is spun from this moment: the themes are usually family, care, and Patrick's favorite: lost-and-found narratives.

The Ankylo is on her side: she bleats, her tail thumps. I have a flashback to my mom lying help-less on a gurney, and have to push that image away.

"Mrs. Leiss?" says Sandy.

"Yes, honey?"

"Mrs. Leiss, when Patrick radios, I get scared."

"Why?" I look at her in the rearview. Sandy has flyaway hair and panicked green eyes: it always confuses me how her face translates to the screen.

"I worry we'll have to do scary things."

Sandy has become very sensitive since her mom died, so I go gently. "That's natural, honey," I say. "But we all have to do things we don't want. The choice is how you react. And you might as well be positive, because Patrick's not going to stop calling. Which is a good thing. Otherwise we'd be out of a job!"

Patrick signals, and we head out of the car tracked by the cameras and the microphones.

The Ankylo looks awful. Hundreds of maggots explore a stomach lesion. Her vent is red with an infection, and the male has crushed a hind leg. Mating is always dangerous for the female.

"Ick!" says Sandy, inspecting the wound.

This is now Sandy's standard reaction to all dino injury, and it's very dull. It would be less boring if she could just use different words. Mol has started copying her, and it drives me insane.

"The maggots eat meat," I say, "you eat meat. No difference."

"I'm not a maggot," says Sandy, with her open, troubled face. "And besides, there is such a thing as a *stove*."

"We'll say she's lost her family," says Patrick, unmiked. "We'll say she got separated."

Patrick always uses this as a stand-in when mating's gone wrong: here's the mom, he'll say, here's the poppa, here's the babas, even though he knows the carnivores would just as soon scarf their own babies.

I check the dino's vitals. "Know why baby dinos don't mewl for their mothers, girls?"

"Why?"

"Because if they made even a noise they'd soon be mommy's lunch."

Mol laughs, and brings a bucket from the pond. She lets the Ankylo's blue tongue lap at the water. The boom mic swings overhead.

"Careful you don't get rabies or something," says Sandy.

I give her a look that means: say something appropriate.

"She's so cute," Sandy says.

"Remember when we came here for that picnic?" I say to Patrick, away from the mike.

"Sure," he says.

I give the Ankylo a tranquilizer, then a truckload of antibiotic. There's no transport, so we'll have to hope Toro won't find her tonight. Maybe Patrick, feeling lenient, will throw him some turkeys and not let him out.

"What if Toro gets her?" says Sandy, looking at Patrick.

"Toro can pick on someone his own size," I say, which is meaningless, but whatever.

Mol looks pale and I see she is crying. One of the cameramen tightens the lens on her face. "Hey, baby," I say, gathering her in my arms. Though we doctor dinos all the time in Eden Park, I have always been careful to shield Mol from their deaths. "Don't worry. Patrick says she'll be fine."

Sandy wants to take a selfie with Mol and the Ankylo. "Sad face," says Sandy. Neither of them smile. Quietly, out of earshot of Patrick—though not, I fear, the boom mike—she says to Mol: "I hate this fucking park."

I look to Patrick but he hasn't heard. Dropping F-bombs like this is pretty dumb; especially for someone hanging on a live wire, as Sandy is. Sandy was born here—a real lifer—and should, frankly, know better.

Patrick gives me this look that means—go put

your arm around Sandy, like you just did with Mol. I bring them both toward me until the camera stops rolling and then let go. "Watch your mouth," I say to Sandy.

"OK, Claire," says Patrick, "do your thing."

They never show this part. I palpate the Ankylo's backside. Though she's knocked out, she still kicks with my hand so high in her vent. At last I find her eggs; pearlescent, thin-shelled, immensely warm.

All of us Mrs. moms live in cabins in the compound, fenced off from the dino enclosures. All the homes are identical: everything is pine and plaid. It's a little homely for my taste, but it looks good on-screen, with the shotguns and the mounted moose heads. Even the judgy online moms sometimes say nice things about the décor in the Comments.

My mom always liked cozy spaces: she always said "home is the nicest thing there is." I could imagine that embroidered on a cushion—though that was never her thing. She wasn't a cliché bouncy person; she actively worked for her outlook. To be honest, for a long time after Dad left, she was a mess; just as I was, after her.

At home that evening Patrick calls. "I liked that moment at the end." His voice is mellow, beautiful.

"It was touching, when you put your arm around Sandy. You looked like a new family."

When he uses these words about emotion he's actually talking audience metrics. Despite this, sometimes I wonder if Patrick is flirting with me, though I always doubt whether I can call these things: romantically, I've had so many failures that I never know when my judgment is off. After all, I read Mol's dad as a safe bet, and he left before Mol was even born. Things were too intense, he said: the baby, your dead mom, you know?

"It made me think you could be, like, *de facto* mom to Sandy?"

"*De facto* mom?"

"Look, Mrs. Appleton's on the skids. She's no good. Can't Sandy room with you? The fans want to see Sandy taken care of. Re-integrated. It makes perfect sense. What with the sick Ankylo-mom and the new Ankylo babies to come. It'll be our adoption episode!"

"What would I do with her?"

"Pajama parties! Brunch! I don't know. Whatever makes girls happy. You're the momma: you know best. Let her sleep over for a few days. I'll tell Mrs. A. to bring over her stuff."

The girls are drawing at the table. They always

draw unicorns, never dinos: bodies leaping, tales erect; their eyelashes big as jetties. "Want to stay for dinner, Sandy?"

The kitchen cam tightens on the girls.

"What are you having?"

Pure Sandy: gift horse, mouth.

"Turkey drumsticks."

"Sure," she says, "OK."

Overnight I hear Toro rage. ROAR! *ROAR!* We get it, I want to say: you're sad in your aloneness, but please, PLEASE, please could you let us get some sleep?!

I should be used to it by now but the stink from Toro's poop in the mornings is awful. When I worked with domestic companions I'd be retching all the time: yeast infections, fluid boluses, blocked anal glands. People don't realize what the skin keeps in! All the moms here try to pretend it's nothing worse than the creamiest baby diaper they've ever dealt with, but the scent is awful and coats everything. Frankly, it makes me want to barf, but in front of Mol I pretend I'm not affected, because I don't want her to overthink Toro, Mrs. Cooper, etcetera.

When the girls are at school the next day I drive to the watering hole. All that's left of the Ankylo is darkened sand. Probably she's gone somewhere to die, or, more likely, has been eaten. Her disappearance grieves me. I don't think I did right by her. I should have given her a "soft goodbye" with ketamine and barbiturates, but I didn't want to do it in front of Mol, lest the endless death starts to become a thing, and besides, I left my old job because I didn't want to do that anymore.

My mom at one point also asked me to slip her something.

"I can't," I said, and soon she resumed her cheer, and we both pretended it hadn't happened.

On my tablet I report the Anyklo is no longer at the GPS location. Likely dead, I write.

And so Sandy begins to stay over. In the mornings the girls head to the schoolhouse. At night we eat turkey patties and soft serve while watching *La Fortuna,* a period drama set in sixteenth-century Spain. After the show they share a bath. Though they're both too old for this, it's not in fact that weird: the bathroom is "neutralized" by sitting on the toilet, or getting into the water, because the contracts won't let the kids be shown naked. It's good they know what space is "live" and which "dead"—otherwise they'd be walking around with two selves; totally confused.

Now it's Sandy who shares Mol's bed. I feel a little sad that I have to say good night then withdraw, but it's OK. We're temporarily housing an orphan, I say to myself, Sandy won't be here forever. I haven't yet mentioned that I'm the new "mom," but Sandy seems happy enough.

So I start to think that maybe Patrick's right. I *am* a natural! Sandy has been in my house for less than three days and already she's doing better! Patrick says he's super happy with our home footage. And even when Sandy is grievous I'm super breezy, and just aerosol her sadness away: "Mrs. Leiss, sometimes when I see Toro poop I wonder if it has my mom in it." (And I say: "Come on, Sandy! Let's look on the bright side. Your mom wouldn't have wanted you to be unhappy.") "But I don't want to die because of Toro!" ("Baby, Toro is behind a hundred-foot electric fence!") "Except at night." ("Except at night," I say, "when we are.")

And I think that maybe this is not so bad. That I'm doing a good job as a retrofit Mrs. Cooper. Maybe better? You know, the thing about Sandy's mom was that she was a notorious spender, always coming home with bags of toys because she felt bad about Sandy growing up on a dinoranch—which is dumb, because if she had really felt bad, she might have set

Sandy up with a trust fund instead, and in fact might have thought twice about screwing Patrick up at the watchtower. I try to ask Sandy about her mom, but when I do the lights go out and I think maybe she will say something terrible. *Who?*

Now that the show's theme is "caring for the lost and found," Patrick has asked me to steer the girls toward looking after the eggs, which isn't hard, since they're already very interested. We keep the eggs warm in a cage with fresh dry hay. When the girls come home from school they baby-talk them. "You're OK," they say. "Momma's back." Mol sings them lullabies, sweetly out of tune. They name the eggs after *La Fortuna* characters: Isabella (of Castile), Juana (of Portugal). Patrick says it's just ideal, all of this material. He says they're going to break with the naming convention and call this show "Mrs. Leiss and the Lost Little Ones."

With our three new arrivals it feels as if we too are nesting.

For each episode we film a brand-sponsored moment. Usually this is with food or a beverage, or unpackaging toys. Since kids empath better with other kids, usually it's Mol alone opening the product, but this week Patrick has asked if I can introduce both girls to the sponsored soda. These moments are a little more choreo'd than usual.

"So this one is peach-flavored. What do you think? Kind of a cool flavor, huh?"

"Hmm," says Mol, sipping at the drink, which gives off a fermenty spritz. "What's it called?"

"Kombucha."

"Calvados?" Mol says, plucking the word from nowhere. "Calvados!"

"It's called kombucha."

Mol shouts, "Calvados! Calvados! I love CALVADOS!"

"Calvados is a brandy. This is *kombucha*." I'm a bit more stern because Patrick won't like her mentioning alcohol.

Sandy grabs the bottle and swigs. "I love you too, Calvados!"

Mol grabs another bottle from the fridge and swigs from it too. They're drinking it so fast that it's making them burp. *Burp* goes one, and then the other. Lurching around the room, the girls look juiced.

"It's good for your tummy," I say calmly. "Makes you poop," I say, instantly regretful.

Mol positions the bottle below her butt. "I've pooped Calvados!"

Now Sandy is cracking up, and the high jinks are

escalating rather than leveling off. *Burp*; then, *poop, poop!* Calvados, Calvados!

All of this is unusable, and I need to find a way to quiet them down so that we can restart. I widen my eyes as if I'm suddenly scared. It takes awhile for the girls to notice ("*Poop, fart,* Calvados!"), but when they do, I make my breath quicker. I make sure I've got their full attention, then turn to the window, where there is a reflection of our spectral family.

"TORO!!!" I shout, smashing a plate to the floor for extra effect.

The girls scream, looking truly terrified, then I burst out laughing. "Only yoking!" I say, pointing to the eggs, but by then Sandy has already rushed to the bathroom, where she stays for some time.

Really, the girls' faces! Sometimes doing this show is just so much fun.

The next morning Sandy is unfortunately back to her suboptimal self. Our honeymoon is over, and, to make matters worse, one of the eggs—Isabella of Castile, they tell me—is a write-off. The kitchen is suddenly a plague house; the smell, intolerable.

I ask Sandy to put the dud in the trash. She keeps her foot on the pedal; her pale eyes swim. When she lifts her foot the can closes, making a cymbal sound as if someone has made a joke.

"C'mon now, Sandy. You'd hardly say a prayer for a fried egg."

The small muscles in her jaw clench.

To be honest, I'm annoyed more at myself. Any vet would tell you not to get attached. Try losing a dog, a cat, a sheep, a horse—then you'll understand an unhatched egg is nothing but an IOU for the future. The other egg actually looks more promising; tiny movements come from within.

"I'm sorry," I say to the girls.

"For what?" Sandy asks.

"For the egg."

"Whatever," Sandy says, her eyes going to the window.

I have apologized to Patrick about the kombucha, and he said it wasn't a problem; the girls were having fun, but I could tell he wasn't being honest. For hours Sandy wouldn't come out of the bathroom after my prank. Now there are dark rings under her eyes. Perhaps Toro kept her awake. He was particularly vigorous last night (ROAR, ROAR; *GNASH, GNASH*) which was bad timing after my joke.

I really don't like the idea of Sandy sharing a bed with Mol if she is up all night tossing and turning.

"Are you tired, Mol?" I say, stroking her hair. "You look tired."

"No," she says.

I think about decanting Sandy to the sofa bed downstairs.

"This is bad," she says. There's a glitter in Sandy's eye. She looks around the room as if seeing it for the first time. "Oh, this is worse than before."

In vet school we learned how baby lab rats lose their heat, sleep less, and utter a nonstop ultrasonic cry when separated from their mothers. I try to bear this in mind when it comes to Sandy; that she might need some time, just as I did. "Hey, hey. Where's that attitude going to get you, Sand?" I bring her in to me but it doesn't feel quite right, so I kiss the crown of her head to signal we're finished.

"Yeah, can you not, actually?" Sandy says. "You have very bad breath."

Mol watches for my reaction, but I won't be baited by an eleven-year-old who's so delusional she can eat bacon for breakfast yet grow disconsolate over an egg. Besides, I've seen enough suboccipital tumors in enough mutts to think maybe Sandy's new behavior might be limbic.

"What's gotten into you? I thought we were having a nice time."

"We were," she says.

Sandy's force field today is 100 percent negative, and I can feel myself giving in to its pull, which is a direction I have absolutely chosen not to follow. "Wanna do Calvados?" I say, pulling a bottle from the fridge.

"No," they both say, in time.

After school the girls are in the yard, digging up dirt. I check the trash; Isabella is no longer there. For a terrible moment I remember taking home my mother's clothes from the hospital and putting them in the trash too.

Out in the yard the two girls are dressed in lace mantillas: they look like the merchant wives of the *conquistadores*. I want to laugh; they might have ridden in on horses. Are they singing? Chanting? Burying the warrior dead? When they come in their eyes are puffy.

"*¿Qué occure?*" I ask, but they don't answer, and go straight to Mol's room.

"Hey," I text Patrick.

Three dots, which then go. I'm pretty sure he's still angry about the kombucha, even though he says he isn't. Knowing he's pissed with me makes me pissed at Sandy. While I wait for a reply I make up the sofa bed. I wonder what the acoustics will be like downstairs, with Toro so close.

"You're up for filming soon," Patrick writes, finally. This is code for a Toro shoot. It might be punishment for the sponsored moment gone bad.

"OK," I write back.

Under the Toro episodes the moms in the Comments always ask how I can bear to put Mol in danger. They don't know that the most she's sustained in four years has been a day of dehydration, some tick bites, a touch of sunstroke. I figure it's like this: driving a car—very dangerous! Probably the thing most likely to kill you. And yet we all do it, all the time. Toro: very dangerous. But the Jeep: probably more so.

Anyway, I'm sure this critique is from the same parents who let their kids watch our show outside of the Kids portal. A friend once told me that after the season finale the algorithm eventually scrolled to something pornographic. So, you know, danger is relative. Watch us in the Kids portal, we say over and over, but mom is already on her phone, posting photos of her kids on Instagram, or Facebook, or whatever.

When we first joined Eden Park, Mol was amazed at the fauna roaming the ranch; the dinos enormous and multicolored, as if dipped in Crayolas. Personally, I was thrilled I'd finally made a good decision as her mom. Now, I could see her all day. She was even part of my work.

At the animal hospital I'd put in twelve-hour shifts and only see Mol for a minute in the evenings. Plus, all I did was euthanize animals—putting pooches to sleep all day, it was like *Consummatum Est* 24/7 in there. Anyway, that's why I gave up domestic companions and came here instead.

Yes, I kept thinking, in my first few days out in the Jeep, with the cobalt sky throwing hard shadows from the land—this is my life?! I had never thought of myself as pretty enough for TV, and vets aren't exactly in high demand for reality shows. And yet, when we arrived, I saw we were made for this place. Mol began to thrive. And so did I.

One day, a few weeks in, we were picnicking by the watering hole—me, Patrick, and Mol—when a herd of Parasauralophus—basically bigger, cuter Iguanodons—came over to drink. The light was pink, violet; the shot—later, when I saw it—had the feel of a nature documentary in the Serengeti. I looked to Patrick, who was so handsome in the rosy light, then to Mol, and I realized what I felt was profound happiness; and that Mol might just be the deepest expression of loveliness I'd ever made.

It is one of my life's regrets that my mom never met her. She died while I was pregnant, and the smell of the chemo ward—like something wet but also burnt through—was enough to heap nausea onto nausea. I didn't want to go near her and yet, when she was gone, I couldn't bear the fact she was no longer here. I spent a lot of time being unhappy and I think I radiated that, which wasn't really fair on Mol.

When I came to Eden Park, I made a conscious decision. Enough was enough. No more twelve-hour shifts; no more lonely Mol; no more centrifugal dead-mom-grief. Eden Park was a paradise, and I brightened significantly.

Over the next week Sandy's negativity continues, and Mol too starts sulking. When Mol doesn't like something now she says it's "sebaceous." When I kiss her goodnight she says: "Yeah, can you not? You have very bad breath."

The one good thing to come out of all of this is that Patrick is now in constant communication. Sometimes, listening to his voice, I can understand why Mrs. Cooper traversed the ranch in the dark without a gun. Sometimes, I think he's about to say: Claire, why don't you come over for a glass of Cabernet? It's lonely up here on my own.

He asks me to try to improve their mood. The footage is doomy, he says: the audience doesn't want Sandy's sad mug, or need any reminding that her mother was chomped by the park's apex predator.

But honestly I get nowhere, and soon it's both girls who are unspeaking. Now every morning there's a *funeral* in the kitchen. Not a word! Do you want toast, girls? Cheerios? Pop-Tarts? Viennoiserie? Huevos rancheros? Do you want any of this food I have been *slaving* over, trying to make you happy?

Nothing!

I tell myself this is a phase. A phase, Claire! Outwaiting it is the only approach, and what you have to remember with kids is how *rubbery* they are. "They'll bounce back," my mom would have said. "Just give them time."

Soon, though, there's another problem: Juana of Portugal is going green. There's a pressure inside the egg, and a tightness to the shell. She stinks. Worse, the girls won't even acknowledge what's happening. "Juana's so cute," they say to each other. "Such a sweet Ankylo!"

Rotten albumen can spurt five or six feet. The force is intense, like your waters breaking—which I guess is the same thing? When they hold Juana I fear it will fire into their eyes.

I text Patrick. "Is this long term? Sandy being here?"

No reply.

I always imagined Sandy would "graduate" to somewhere else after here.

I take a walk to Mrs. Appleton's cabin. Somewhere close, a Sauropod lows from the herbivore pen. It's a beautiful sound: religious; almost Abrahamic. They are majestic creatures. Once upon a time Mol and I used to doughnut their legs with our Jeep.

Mrs. Appleton is smoking a cigarette on the porch. Bullfrogs join the cicadas, but there's no Toro, not yet.

I say it might be better if Sandy were to return to her cabin.

"I can't force her," Mrs. Appleton says, shrugging.

She looks intoxicated and I wonder what she's on. All vets I've ever known skim a little, though I have no idea how Mrs. A. can measure molar quantities of gabapentin for herself when the dosage is for a sixty-ton Brachio. Apparently she used to be a committed Christian, but all of that finished when her daughter left and stopped speaking to her.

"Do you know if Sandy has other family?"

"She has an aunt, I think. In Westville?"

I look through the fence. I wonder if I can see a pair of burning eyes heading toward us. Mrs. A. stubs out her cigarette on the decking.

"Be careful," I say. "Wildfires."

"You think *that's* what's going to get us?" Mrs. Appleton lies down on her porch. Something about her concentrated aloneness makes me think she won't ever be taking Sandy back. Sandy, in fact, will be mine for ever.

Mrs. Appleton's nostrils wing as she takes another smell, lofted in on the breeze. "I swear it's like an aphrodisiac, sometimes, that stench."

And I think she might be right: deep inside it, a hint of truffle.

And then, Christ alive! Juana of Portugal splats all over the hay. The reek is awful. I ask the girls if they want to do the funny burial thing in the garden again—I tell them I'll get out the fancy dress—but Sandy just throws Juana in the trash. Mol winces.

"I'm sorry I couldn't keep it alive," I say. "I am. But really so much is beyond my control here."

Sandy looks at her uneaten toast.

"You're upset about the egg," I say. "I get it."

"No, you don't," says Sandy. "I know the Ankylo died too. I saw it on your tablet."

"Mom?" says Mol, shocked. "Is that true?"

"Things die, Sandy."

"No, things die *here*." She looks to Mol, who already looks scared enough. "Would *you* let your daughter grow up on a dinoranch, Mol? Where any moment you might be—"

"Enough! Mol, go to your room."

"No."

"*Now*."

It's a slow protest, but she gets there eventually. I myself am trying to hold my cool, though the smell from the egg is ultra-nauseating; plus, gigantic emojis of Toro turd are mulching the back field, which is enough to make your eyes water.

I switch off the kitchen camera.

"What are you doing?" Sandy says, alarmed.

"OK, Sandy, how do you want to play this? Want me to tell Patrick that you're not playing ball? That you're not star material anymore? He's already upset about the kombucha. Do you even *want* to be here?"

"What choice do I have?"

"Ample choice! Ample choice! Your aunt in Westville, for example. I'm sure she'd have you."

Sandy puts her head in her hands. "This is all I've ever known."

"Then participate. Pretend."

"How?"

"We are happy here. OK? You are spoiling this for us."

"I am *spoiling* this for you?"

"Yes! Yes, you are!"

Sandy narrows her eyes. "You're a dinosaur, Mrs. Leiss."

"Oh, please. I feel bad about Isabella, and Tiana."

"Juana."

"Whatever."

"You don't feel bad about me, though," Sandy says. "What am *I* meant to do here? With you? With all of this? With that thing, out there?"

I just cannot find it in myself to therapize Sandy and single-mom Mol: this is not, I think, my burden. And—perfect timing—Toro finds this moment to let out a rancorous cry. He's usually asleep in the day, but if he's this active now it means today we'll film in his pen. I wonder if Sandy's smell will be familiar to him.

Without warning, Sandy barfs onto her plate. Since the girls haven't eaten in days I can't believe she has anything to even bring up. The smell makes me want to barf too, but the daisy chain of puking has to stop, so I slide Sandy's plate into the trash and take it out to the garbage.

Outside the air is musty. Despite this I take big gulps to clear my head. Sandy's misery, her feelings: they are all too much.

Mrs. A. is rocking in the porch swing. "Today's the day," she shouts.

"Sure is!"

"Good luck," she says. "He sounds enthusiastic already!"

I wave and go back inside.

Sandy is still in the same spot. I wonder if, around her, there might be that ultrasonic cry that I too gave off, non-stop, for so long after my mother went.

Another roar from Toro makes a shudder go right through Sandy. I know what she wants me to say. Even Patrick wants me to say it: that I acknowledge her as mine. But I can't, and I don't want to.

The radio in the den buzzes. "Claire?" It's Patrick.

Sandy is very pale. "Why is Toro out already?"

"Claire. Come in? You're up."

I head to the den but Sandy holds my arm. Her hand is small and so cold. "I didn't mean it," she says. "What I said before. I'm sorry. Please."

"Thank you, Sandy. For apologizing."

"You won't make me go, will you? I can't do a shoot with Toro," she says. "I just can't, Mrs. Leiss."

"That's up to you, honey," I say, since it's always up to us, isn't it, what we do with our pain? "That's up to you. It's always been one hundred percent your choice."

Sandy looks at me, her eyes flooded.

"So," I say. "What will it be?"

Acknowledgments

My friend Andrew Cowan taught me how to write a story, and how, more importantly, to write these stories. I can't really thank him enough.

A huge thank-you to my agent extraordinaire, Cathryn Summerhayes—what a formidable force you are! And here for me through thick and thin. Thank you so much to Rebecca Gradinger and Sarah Fuentes at Fletcher and Co/UTA. Gratitude to the whole team at Curtis Brown UK: Georgie Mellor, Jazz Adamson, Annabelle White, and Jess Molloy.

I am so grateful to Francesca Main for always championing my work and being the best of editors. I couldn't be luckier in having you. At Orion, thank you to Aoife Datta, Yadira Da Trindade, Susie

Bertinshaw, Jake Alderson, and Sandra Taylor (*per sempre*). Special thanks to Dan Jackson, who invoked vintage Nora Ephron in the beautiful cover design.

Thank you so much to Katherine Nintzel at William Morrow and Clara Sondermann at HarperCollins for being such joyous champions of my work in the U.S. and Germany.

Thank you to Jonathan Beckman, Yan Ge, Kathleen McCaul Moura, and Ben Pester, who offered their insights on early drafts; as well as the support of the Creative Writing department at UEA, and my "Coven." Thank you to Sarah Hall for so much early enthusiasm in approaching the story as a form.

Thank you to directors Klaudia Reynicke and Chris Andrews, who offered their expertise with "Dracula at the Movies"; Carla MacKinnon and Greg Buchanan for their video games advice in "Lesley, in Therapy"; Gabri Liotta and Julia Lubomirska for checking the Italian and French.

Thank you to Jonathan Calascione for supporting my creativity from another world to my own.

Thank you to all the *freghi* who let me work on this book at the Civitella Ranieri Foundation in Umbria, six years later than planned.

Love and gratitude to my family: Pamela, Michael, and Katherine Wood; to Hannah Nixon, Alaina

Wong, and Eve Williams. My other family: Philippa, Fran, Gabi, and Letitia Harkness. And always in my thoughts: William.

And, last but not least, my loves—Ed, Joanie, and Ari.

I promise none of these stories are about you.

ABOUT

MARINER BOOKS

MARINER BOOKS traces its beginnings to 1832 when William Ticknor cofounded the Old Corner Bookstore in Boston, from which he would run the legendary firm Ticknor and Fields, publisher of Ralph Waldo Emerson, Harriet Beecher Stowe, Nathaniel Hawthorne, and Henry David Thoreau. Following Ticknor's death, Henry Oscar Houghton acquired Ticknor and Fields and, in 1880, formed Houghton Mifflin, which later merged with venerable Harcourt Publishing to form Houghton Mifflin Harcourt. HarperCollins purchased HMH's trade publishing business in 2021 and reestablished their storied lists and editorial team under the name Mariner Books.

Uniting the legacies of Houghton Mifflin, Harcourt Brace, and Ticknor and Fields, Mariner Books continues one of the great traditions in American bookselling. Our imprints have introduced an incomparable roster of enduring classics, including Hawthorne's *The Scarlet Letter,* Thoreau's *Walden,* Willa Cather's *O Pioneers!,* Virginia Woolf's *To the Lighthouse,* W.E.B. Du Bois's *Black Reconstruction,* J.R.R. Tolkien's *The Lord of the Rings,* Carson McCullers's *The Heart Is a Lonely Hunter,* Ann Petry's *The Narrows,* George Orwell's *Animal Farm* and *Nineteen Eighty-Four,* Rachel Carson's *Silent Spring,* Margaret Walker's *Jubilee,* Italo Calvino's *Invisible Cities,* Alice Walker's *The Color Purple,* Margaret Atwood's *The Handmaid's Tale,* Tim O'Brien's *The Things They Carried,* Philip Roth's *The Plot Against America,* Jhumpa Lahiri's *Interpreter of Maladies,* and many others. Today Mariner Books remains proudly committed to the craft of fine publishing established nearly two centuries ago at the Old Corner Bookstore.